WHAT PEOPLE ARE SAYING ABOUT JOHN H. SIBLEY

"In *Being and Homelessness*, John does a fantastic evocation of the space in his stories and really makes me understand why Maxwell Street was so important to so many people."

Jason Pettus
Chicago Center of
Literature and Photography

"*Darwin's Ghetto* is a page-turning read that will leave you thinking about the ethics of biology/genetic engineering, and most importantly, the hard realities of smart young men struggling to grow up and thrive in an environment plagued by violence, racism and poverty."

Bella Franco

"*Darwin's Ghetto* is stark, riveting and bleak. It is a portrait of genius gone awry by a thirst for revenge."

Kevin Lintner

"I feel like *Darwin's Ghetto* opened my mind to the thought process of a circumstantially disturbed, yet genius, dramatic-minded boy whom experienced a terrible and much too common family tragedy."

Katie

[On HEX] "Sibley weaves many of the things we consider myths, urban legends, and wives' tales into a statement that says 'could supernatural occurrences fall into the realm of science after all?'"

Stephen – Goodreads

"To keep me reading is truly saying something."

John W. Fountain
New York Times

"Sibley shows us in BODYSLICK that a futuristic Chicago is not for the timid."

Rollie Welch
Library Journal Editor

"With creative writers like Sibley, the sky is the limit."

Rob Kenner
VIBE Fiction Editor

"Bodyslick is set in a vividly detailed version of modern day Chicago."

Sam Feldman
Chicago Weekly

"*The Color of My Blood* is a stark look at what it's like to be different in such a harsh world. John Sibley's amazing words jump right out at you. Hard to stop reading!"

Lunabea, editor

"If you love Southern gothic fiction you will love HEX"

Bella Franco

"USS OBAMA 2112 is an anthology by John H. Sibley that is truly original and not similar to anything I have read before. While writing some very well-researched science-fiction, he also tackles a lot of issues that many writers are afraid to even mention, especially racial conflict. His voice is a strong one that needs to be heard.

The stories in this collection were a pleasure to read, and John H. Sibley has gained, not only a fan in me, but someone who will tell anyone who will listen about his visionary work. The world needs more writers like him."

Craig Herndon
Editor for Beyond Science Magazine

Published by:
John Sibley at SIBSARTSTUDIO
2015.

All rights are reserved. Without limiting the rights under copyright reserved above, no part of this publication may be reproduced, stored in or introduced into a retrieval system, or transmitted, in any form, or by any means (electronic, mechanical, photocopying, recording, or otherwise) without the prior written permission of the author.

©SIBSARTSTUDIO 2015.

American citizenship should not be like a Cracker Jack prize. Read The Senate debate over what became the 14th Amendment to the constitution and learn about its architects' intentions, which was to guarantee equal rights for recently freed slaves and their children. It was also a rebuke to The Dred Scott decision, which declared that African-Americans were not and could not be citizens of the United States, and to article 1, Section 2 of the U.S. Constitution of 1787, which said that for the purpose of representation in Congress, enslaved blacks in a state would be counted

*For my granddaughters,
Jordyn and Kennedy*

A proof

The clause "subject to the jurisdiction thereof" that it meant "not owing allegiance to anybody else and being subject to the complete jurisdiction of the United States."

(the 3 fifths Compromise)
(count 3 of 5 slaves as a person)
"as three fifths of all other persons."
This is why "original intent" is important.

(The Three-fifths-Compromise was a compromise between Southern and Northern states reached during the Philadelphia Convention of 1787

CONTENTS

Bug Light 1

THE COLOR OF MY BLOOD 15

USS OBAMA 2112 57

DARWIN'S GHETTO 95

HEX 151

Hangar 17 179

Acknowledgements 213

About the Author 214

BUG LIGHT

March 3, 1898

Dr. George Washington Carver

Tuskegee University

I was riding my horse-driven wagon to nearby farms to teach farmers how legumes-peanuts, peas, and beans all have a symbolic relationship with bacteria. Bacteria that can take nitrogen molecules from the atmosphere and convert them into a form plants could use. I wanted the farmers to understand that they had to look at the entire natural system for them to become efficient and profitable.

While I was riding back to my lab at Tuskegee, I had the most astonishing thoughts as I watched the twinkling lightning bugs. Even when I was about 12 years old and walking eight miles to school in Neosho, Missouri, in the dark, I was always delighted in the fireflies' glow, and I was curious about the chemistry of these insects. But now, I viewed them as a trained scientist, wondering if it was possible to develop organic lights in plants using the same chemical reaction that lightning bugs used.

I leaped out of the wagon and opened a peanut jar that had a lid punched with holes. I caught about 30 of the bugs and took them back to my lab.

Since my youth, I've always been intrigued with their glow. The reason a firefly's glow will stay etched in my memory is that in 1888, when I was 14 years old, I moved to Fort Scott, Kansas, to continue my education. This was about 75 miles from my hometown of Neosho. I got a job with the Payne family as a cook. They were very kind, white folks, even though there was racial prejudice in the town. I remember running an errand for the Payne family, trying to catch fireflies while I walked. That's when I spotted an angry white mob pull a black prisoner from the Fort Scott jail. Blind terror etched on his coal-black face.

The rays of a blood-red moon filtered through tall Oakwood trees, casting a ghastly shadow on the jailhouse. The night air was thick and humid. A lone wolf and a pack of dogs barked with a mouthful cadence. The hoot of a barn owl echoed ominously and crickets chirped. Blinking lights of the fireflies casted an eerie demonic mood to the scene. Bats lurched from trees, plucking bugs out of midair.

The white mob started beating the prisoner with bricks, tree branches, and lumber. I heard the crack of his skull and bones as they were crushed from the blows. A sheet of blood cascaded over his cracked skull. A wrenching falsetto moan cut through the night air. The mob had beaten him to death. I stood there, frozen with disbelief as they dragged the mangled body to the public square and set it on fire.

The whites gathered around his burning body as if they were at a picknick (pick a nigger). Children poked sticks at his burning body, causing flickering tongues of flame to leap from it. A man snatched off one of the charred ears. I heard his flesh sizzle like bacon in a frying pan. The stench of the burning flesh still clings to me. I will never forget the terrible night and the glow of the firefly light. The naked horror and barbarity of that murder has haunted me my entire life.

In March 1896, I received a letter from Booker T.

Washington, the founder and principal of Tuskegee Institute, an African-American school in Tuskegee, Alabama. At the time, I was the first African-American student at Iowa State College. I had to write a thesis. I actually wrote two; one dealt with the crossbreeding of plants to create new hybrids. The title was "Plants as Modified by Man." The purpose of crossbreeding was to continue the best qualities of two different plants to create a new, more desirable plant. In one experiment, I crossed a scarlet geranium with the chemical of a firefly to produce a plant with glowing salmon-colored blossoms. I wrote a second thesis titled, "Organic Light in Plants."

After accepting the teaching position of Tuskegee, I always started my day with early walks through the woods and the countryside. On those walks, I always took my botany can - my peanut jar with holes in the lid - and a carrying strap for gathering specimens. The walks were spiritual to me. They were my way to hear God's plan for me.

- ◊ -

Bug Light Notes

June 3, 1898

If bacteria can take nitrogen molecules from the atmosphere and convert them into a form plants can use, I wonder if the same species of bacteria (which are found in seawater, though they do not emit light) can make peanuts, peas, tobacco, and beans glow. Most bioluminescent animals' photospheres or light-producing cells are restricted and only glow on a specific surface.

June 5, 1898

I have an aquarium in my lab with an assortment of bioluminescent fish, but I was astonished after dissecting a pineapple fish to find that there is a single light organ containing bioluminescent; bugs, such as fireflies, have different locations for light cells when they are larvae and when they are adults.

- ◊ -

While teaching at Tuskegee, I wrote letters to keep in contact with friends I made while at Simpson College and Iowa State College. One of those friends was my mentor and former professor.

Dr. Louis B. Banzel

Mycology Department

Iowa State College

March 30, 1897

> *I'm enjoying my work very much indeed here, teaching at Tuskegee. It's indeed a different world compared to Iowa. I'm interested in what you think about my, "Organic Light Plant Theory." You are an expert in chemistry, mycology, the study of fungi, and plant diseases. I'm interested in how you think my glowing plants could be used in the industry.*
>
> *God bless*

Bug Light Notes

June 3, 1909

In my laboratory, I had been working on developing a new cotton hybrid. It would combine the best qualities of short stalk and tall-stock cotton. In 1910, I introduced my new hybrid; I called it Carver's Hybrid.

In 1916, I was elected a fellow of England's Royal Society of Arts, Manufacturers, and Commerce. I was the first African-American to be recognized by that organization. To think I was a former slave, and now a member of the Royal Society. Sometimes I have to pinch myself to make sure this is happening to me.

That award led to the attention of the great inventor, Thomas Edison. Edison was interested in my research in producing rubber from the sweet potato. I had also sent him my theory on "Organic Plant Light" by mistake. We had a lot in common; like me, he had a garden with thousands of tropical plants in his Florida home. He has a special botanical laboratory filed with potted plants that his botanists were trying to crossbreed.

Rubber was one of the most critical commodities of the modern industrial world. But the problem was it could only be produced in distant tropical climates. The Edison Botanic Research Company was created in 1927 with the Ford Motor Company and the Firestone Tire & Rubber Company. Edison's "hunts" for some plant developed by crossbreeding that could produce rubber led him to my lab at Tuskegee. He offered me a huge salary to work with him for five years in his laboratory in West Orange, New Jersey. I told him I couldn't leave Tuskegee.

May 5, 1909

I've been dissecting and studying fireflies for the past 10 years. I have discovered that fireflies and glowworms regulate their light by controlling the amount of oxygen that reaches light cells via their breathing tubes. There are over 136 species of fireflies, each with a distinctive rate of flashes per second. The flashes are produced by a chemical called luciferase, which they use to attract the opposite sex. Male fireflies perform the light show emitted during summer evenings. I wonder if the luciferin and luciferase could be used one day in research to diagnose and record the size and growth of tumors by injecting the chemical into a patient's bloodstream and then tracing its path through the major organs.

September 4, 1915

Eureka! I've finally created a bioluminescent tobacco plant that will revolutionize the industry. It is unlike the firefly light that is produced by a series of flashes, because the light is under nervous-system control. What I have done is injected a tobacco plant, one of my hybrids with the chemical luciferase, which produces the bugs' light. The difference is a nervous system does not regulate the tobacco light, so it will stay lit until it dies.

I think one of my students sneaked into my basement lab and saw the glowing tobacco plants. He then told the principal, Booker T. Washington, about my research. Washington walked into my lab late in the evening.

He walked close to me and patted my shoulder, grinning as he whispered. "Dr. Carver, you are doing an extraordinary job teaching at the school. We would like to update all of your lab needs. It's just a question of capital. Dr. Carver, a poor Negro school like Tuskegee can't compete in the sciences like white schools."

I nodded my head.

"Dr. Carver, your work could make Tuskegee one of the most famous and richest schools in America!"

"Why, certainly not with work on peanuts?"

"I'm talking about your glowing plants."

"Why...who told you?"

"That's not important. May I see them?"

"Only two people, at least I thought, knew about my glowing plants...apparently there are more."

"I was contacted by an associate of Thomas Edison about the plants. They think it's a hoax. You accidently sent them a thesis on your work. I'm here to prove them wrong. Now, where are the plants?"

"Follow me," I said as I led him down to my small, dark basement lab. As we neared the door, we could see the blue glow of the plants shining beneath it - I unlocked the door and we entered the room.

"Jesus Christ almighty! Dr. Carver, do you realize how revolutionary these plants are? These plants could light homes, factories, and farms. They could compliment the need for electric light. We must immediately patent your theory!"

"No, Principal Washington, I have no need for patents. There are still unknowns about the plants."

"Such as?"

"How long will their light last? Photosynthesis? The effect of organic light on humans?"

"These are mechanical issues," the principal said angrily.

"I tell you, I'm going to contact some powerful investors in the industry to see the plants. If the plants generate light by luminous bacteria as you say...all we need to do is work out the details. Can we shake on this, Dr. Carver?"

"No, but I hope you enjoy the tour!"

As Principal Washington stormed out of the lab and ran up the stairs, I threw water on the plants, destroying their chemical reaction. I only kept one glowing geranium.

In 1926, I hired Ernest Thompson, a young white man, to act as my business manager. It was his job to investigate new opportunities for manufacturing my products.

In March of that year, Carver Products Company was formed. Principal Washington and a group of Atlanta businesspersons organized it. I had shown only these people my actual glowing plants: my business manager, Principal Washington, and Professor Banzel at Iowa State University. The Edison people dismissed my "light theory" as a joke.

In my will, dated May 23, 1932, I wrote that I only had three patents in my life, and I would never apply for a patent for my "Organic Light Theory."

- ◊ -

Bug Light

My name is August N. Bellwood Jr. I was hired as Dr. Carver's lab assistant. I'm a graduate of Cornell University with a Bachelor's Degree in chemistry. I worked with Dr. Carver and he treated me like a son. We had a great working relationship until his death. But I knew the private scientist. He was a scientist who all his life wanted a deep bass voice like Paul Roberson. He told me his high-pitched effete voice has caused him shame and social alienation over the years. He told me that a "Dr. Dick" castrated him when he was 11. He told me he approved of the castration because as a house servant, he did not want to be seen as a threat to the daughter of the slave master.

I believe that Dr. Carver's ideas revolutionized the farm industry. He was way ahead of his time. Today his scientific ideas are called biochemistry.

In 1937, Dr. Carver was invited to speak again at another conference in Dearborn. He met Henry Ford, founder of the Ford Motor Company, who had researchers working on ways to use soybeans in industry.

Publicly, Dr. Carver was an affable, likeable man - a scientist who was a contemporary of such scientific geniuses as Albert Einstein, Thomas Edison, and Nikola Tesla. He was bitter that his early discoveries with bio-fuels were never mentioned as equal to his peers in shaping the course of 20th century American life. He felt that if he had been given the resources and the scourge of racism eliminated, the great debate between Edison and Tesla over the virtues of alternating current (AC) power as opposed to direct current (DC) power would have included his "Organic Light Theory." Dr. Carver felt that if he had the industrial backing like Thomas Edison and Tesla, a fierce battle would have been waged among the three camps. Dr. Carver also felt his "Organic Light Theory" had real-world applications like AC and DC power.

I want to set the record straight that, as his lab assistant, the full extent of his "light experiment" is still not publicly known. All of his papers at the George Washington Carver National Museum in Diamond, Missouri, were confiscated by the U.S. government upon his death, despite the outrage and protest of the George Washington Carver Foundation research board members.

I believe his research on organic light was leaked to the federal government by Edison or Ford, because both of them were curious about using peanuts for products such as gasoline and nitroglycerin, and were especially interested in his research into producing rubber from the sweet potato. Both of them felt if the U.S. entered the war, the foreign rubber supply would be stopped.

Carver's inventions are shrouded in mystery because he never wrote down his formulas. He was very secretive about his work; there are a number of theories on the "lost Carver notebooks" that contained his Organic Light Theory. Theory 1: a secret agency of the federal government confiscated them from his museum. Theory 2: There were not any "lost notebooks." Theory 3: He destroyed his "notebooks" out of rage. Theory 4: I believe his "lost notebooks" are being used for research on "organic light" by a secret government program, as an alternative light energy source. I've been told the government agency is called OLEP; Organic Light Energy Project. After 10 years of working with him, he showed me his only surviving "glowing plant."

One day in December, Carver fell as he entered the Carver Museum. He never fully recovered from the fall. On January 5, 1943, he laid down for a nap and never woke up. I spoke to the doctor that examined his body. He stated he was astonished that "where there should have been testicles, there was nothing but scar tissue."

Introduction to
The Color of My Blood
by David B. Lentz

John Sibley in *The Color of My Blood* takes us back to an era when racism was rampant in America, in the heat of the summer of 1966 in Marquette Park in Chicago.

Damon James is a 325-year-old being who has arrived in Chicago from the Versai Solar System and has no preconceived notions about what he will find in the stark urban culture of America when he is viewed as a "black earthman."

James is in a sense an innocent, in that he wants to understand the ways of earth, but is astounded by the treatment that he finds in Chicago, so foreign to civilized life in his native solar system. In a sense Damon James becomes transformed into an American Adam cast well East of Eden into the bleakest regions of urban Chicago.

Sibley's narrative posture is intriguing as Damon James has no external history of our culture because he is a *tabula rasa,* or blank slate. One sympathizes for this bewildered and innocent gentleman from another world over his impressions of the brutal culture that he encounters in the streets of Chicago.

His outsider status as an alien, in the literary sense of the term, is reminiscent of Jonathan Swift's Gulliver in his travels to new and unfamiliar worlds, and the reactions of Damon James to the culture of Chicago in 1966 almost seem to have literary roots entwined in Swift. Unlike Gulliver, Damon James is a reconstructed human being wearing a plastic exoskeleton, but the new culture to him is not foreign to us.

There is a definite sense of absurdity arising in the Kakfaesque portrayal of Gregor Samsa after he has become a great cockroach in the *Metamorphosis*. In Kafka's classic novel, Gregor earns the spite and revulsion and in rare cases, feelings of empathy from those who knew his former human side through his work or family. So those who love Gregor share the suffering of his transformation from a human being into a great, unwieldy cockroach. Damon James has no one who knew him or loved him in America, nor a native cultural basis for connecting with him in any empathetic way. So James must endure the brazen self-interest and vicious bias that he finds in survival mode in the murderous streets of Chicago.

Because of the innocence of Damon James, Sibley enables us to see a culture that we have experienced or read about in 1966 in Chicago. Dostoevsky used the same narrative technique to great success in his masterpiece, *The Idiot*, in which the protagonist is Prince Myshkin, who is a member of royalty who hardly speaks or needs to do so because the facts of circumstance speak well for themselves. Prince Myshkin simply finds himself constantly in the midst of absurd situations over which he has little control despite his regal powers, and we find ourselves drawn into his point of view by virtue of witnessing it through his bewildered eyes. John Sibley gives us this same winning narrative point-of-view in Damon James, and the writing succeeds because the perspective is novel, endearing, and heart-breaking.

The trip back to 1966 leaves us to beg the question: what has changed since then? Is America at its core really different than it was at the height of the reform which seemed so promising, as multitudes marched in Selma and protested in Grant Park in the sixties? Each reader must come to a personal conclusion as to whether the Chicago, Illinois, of 1966, has made sufficient progress so that it is different from the Ferguson, Missouri, of 2015.

While it's true that a black earthman from Chicago has risen to the highest political office in the land, Ferguson is still Ferguson: the facts of the matter, there and elsewhere, are self-evident in matters of civil rights. Sibley brings new perspective to the discourse of America's progress on civil rights through the experience, insight, and transformation of Damon James into an American Adam.

John Sibley has a gift for new perspective which is evident both in his art and his writing. He revels in finding new ways to perceive reality and his art gives innovative expression to his ability to see life with fresh eyes -- in this case the eyes of an alien named Damon James.

Who among us has never felt the disconnection of existence and separation from the inhumanity of humanity and distance from the bleak artifice of our culture and futility inherent in our civilization? In this sense we understand the absurdity of the existential position in which Damon James finds himself because he is, in reality, no more an alien than we are: he is us.

John Sibley continues his legacy of artistic innovation in *The Color of My Blood,* a portfolio of work destined to linger by virtue of its harsh and honest verisimilitude, blended with and connected to the other-worldliness, which distinguishes him from artistic and literary peers.

John Sibley

THE COLOR OF MY BLOOD

CHAPTER ONE

August 4, 1966

Marquette Park

Chicago, Illinois

My earthman name is Damon James.
I am 31 years old, though on my home planet I am 325. I am from the Versai Solar System, which is many light years from earth. Our scientists have figured out the topology of the universe, which contains a whole network of holes, tunnels, bubbles, webs and bridges that we can travel through. We look at the universe the way earth people look at Swiss cheese: the cheese is space-time and the holes are complex labyrinths that we use to travel to different worlds in the universe.

The earthman body that I am housed in is merely a synthetic external skin. A skin that covers my real 6-foot body, which is scaly, like an alligator, and has 2 arms and bipedal, like humans. It gives me telekinetic ability. My earthian exoskeleton is wired to enable me to speak any galactic language in the solar system, and decode the name of any alien inanimate object visually on any planet. My face would scare the hell out of you: the only creature on earth that it resembles is the Australian frilled lizard; its frills expand around its neck to intimidate that, which threatens it. When mine expand, I kill...the frills also regulate my body temperature on my planet from the scorching heat of a binary star system. I have tendrils hidden under my hat that gives me telekinetic ability and other powers, which are essential for survival on a hostile planet.

I was sent to earth to write, (for the sake of brevity I will use the term "write" even though we use a far superior means of recording our perceptions) a memoir about my interaction with earth culture from a Black earthman's standpoint. Of course, I could have chosen any ethnic group I desired, but the Blacks, because they are the most humiliated on earth, seem the most interesting.

John Sibley

I will never forget the first night I was beamed down to earth. I was unfortunately beamed down on the Southwest side of Chicago, Illinois, which is a terrifying place for a Black earthman to be at night. It was a terrifying situation for anybody to be capriciously tossed into.

"Get that niggggger! Hey nigger, what yah doing over here? This is our turf, nigger!"

I nervously thought: *Nigger? What is a nigger?* Is that what they call Black beings on earth? I was frightened. I have never in all of my galactic travels encountered such blind maniacal hatred. I ducked as a large bottle flew past my head. I peered around frantically for some means of escape as around 50 young White earthmen started running toward me screaming, "White power! White power!"

My three-hearts banged loudly in my young, Black-athletic, synthetic body. To make things even worse, my memory genes were decoded entirely from 20th century earth culture (maybe if my memory genes hadn't been decoded I would have been aware that whites are innately xenophobic). I tried to reason with the maniacal white mob.

"My name is Damon James and I'm —"

It was futile. My tendrils shook vehemently as they reacted to a kaleidoscopic blur of lights popping on inside houses, car horns beeping, glass cracking, shrill voices, and rocks and bricks zooming toward me from every conceivable direction.

I looked around nervously, fear-ridden and in search for some means of escape. It was a dead-end street. I was trapped like a caged animal. A sense of blind hopelessness oozed through my being. I peered up at the milky-black starry sky and wondered if it too late to contact my starship for help. It was. I watched these white beings as they slowly encircled me.

A short white man with a square mustache screamed, "The Nationalist Socialist White People Party has had enough of these black apes coming into our communities! I, Frank Hollins and your leader, ask that this black ape be used as an example of the punishment that niggers will receive for coming into our neighborhood...kill him!"

I stood there petrified with fear. My mind was blank. I felt dizzy. The stars whirled over me. I crouched, I huddled, I moaned, I sweated. They overwhelmed me. They engulfed me. They started to scream and rave at me:

> ---*We're tired of you niggers!*
>
> ---*Niggers and welfare must go!*
>
> ---*What yah' looking for over here? Are you*
>
> *looking for white girls, nigger?*

I wondered if revealing my identity to these sick idiots would save my life. All I had to do was take off my hat and they would fearfully run away. After all, what could be more shocking for a racist white earthman than seeing a so-called nigger with worm-like, writhing, green-tendrils on the top of his head? But I decided not to reveal my true identity; after all, I did request this assignment as a galactic scribe to study earth's culture from the perspective of a black homosapien.

I stood there. My synthetic eyes ticked nervously. Then suddenly they started throwing large rocks, bottles, bricks, and sticks at me. I fell to the ground as a large brick hit me in the thorax; pain shot like hot acid up the whole upper half of my body. I raised my hand trying desperately to protect myself from the onslaught of objects thrown at me.

When I got hit in my synthetic nose, it started to bleed. You must remember that even though I have a synthetic body, I still can feel and react the way my real body would.

I peered at my green blood as it zigzagged down my cheek (the shapers, what we call scientists on Untroz, could not create hemoglobin, an iron-containing red blood pigment; so they created synthetic chlorocruorin, an iron-containing green blood molecule that is blue in its oxygenated form and green when deoxygenated). I immediately covered my face, more concerned about revealing the color of my blood than the flood of objects that were being thrown at me. I started to feel weak and faint as the short leader walked over to my beaten body and started kicking me with a blind, delirious hatred. My limp body tossed back and forth, as I lay semi-conscious; his words echoed through my pain-drenched body.

"Nigger...let this be a lesson to your kind that we, the Nationalist White

People Socialist Party, will eventually exterminate your race!"

I was dizzy, dazed, numb, weak, and nauseated; my weak orbs gazed up at the black sky as stars twinkled down upon me. At that very moment, I felt an overwhelming urge to leave earth and all its primitive racial hang-ups. But "no," I told myself. I have a mission. I must not let this horrible confrontation with a microscopic part of earth's population stop me.

Unceasing pain echoed through my battered being. My grasp of reality started to become fuzzy. I closed my eyes for a moment feeling numb, jangled, and sick. Glistening droplets of green blood oozed from my mouth. I grabbed my hat as it slid from my head. I coiled up into a miserable fetal ball, one hand clutching my hat, the other clapped across my mouth, hiding my blood. I craned my neck and looked at that same face. It was that very same racist face. Damon James, a being that has traveled to all nine of the planets in this solar system was being destroyed by the third. I, Damon James, am a synthetic reconstruction of a black earthman. I am a simulated and sculptured interpretation of a 20th century man being stumped to death by Cro-Magnons.

I watched the earthman leader's foot swing in a wide arc as he started to kick me, when suddenly a strange sound made all of them start to run. It was a whining sound. It hurt my ears. It was like the sensuous moans of the Garsur beings during mating season.

The white leader hollered, "The cops! Let's get outtah heah!"

Cops? I wondered: *What are cops?* Are they some sort of primitive guardian force that protects the common people from hostile forces? Are they a central, state-operated agency that protects alien beings?

I gazed at a blue and white four-wheeled object as it screeched to a stop, pulling up a meter from my pummeled body. As I watched, one white and one black earthman in blue uniforms slammed their vehicle's doors and walked toward me. The lights from their transport system reminded my blurred eyes of a star in supernova.

"Are you alright, sir?" the large blond cop asked as I stood up with his assistance. I again wiped my mouth on my sleeve quickly and grabbed my hat as it slid on my head.

The Color of My Blood

The black cop said, "Brother, don't you know this is Marquette Park, the most racist part of Chicago? Man, are you drunk? You from another planet or something? Don't you know Martin Luther King's protest march just started?"

I wanted to say I was beamed down here from my starship, but how would that have sounded? I said, "I just got lost, that's all. I was, ah, looking for a friend's house and I got confused. You see, I'm not from this plane -city. *James, you had better get your act together,* I thought.

The black cop had smooth brown skin. Grey eyes. He might had been any age from 25 to 35. He looked angered, alert, intelligent and deeply concerned about my welfare. "Now low mister, it's no problem. Do you want to go to the hospital?" The black cop asked.

"Thank you, but no, I am alright, I assure you - just take me to the march."

The black cop looked at me with surprise. "Why you want to join that trouble maker King? Stirring up trouble here in Chicago!"

The car came to a screeching halt as we neared the marchers.

"Be careful!" The cops said as I alighted out of the vehicle.

I ducked as a hailstorm of bottles, bricks and firecrackers were thrown at the marchers. A rock *whooshed* pass my head.

White Power!

There was nearly a thousand blue-helmeted cops. Thousands of white people jeered catcalls at us; many of them waved Nazi flags. Swastikas flapped in the white crowd like the *uhlee* bugs on my planet.

A long black car slowly pulled up to the curb. The police immediately closed in around it. I heard a powerful voice bellow out of the car.

"Let's get out the car Al, this should be a piece of cake compared to *Bloody Sunday* at the Edmund Pettis Bridge in our Selma-to-Montgomery march last year!"

I stood there looking at him. He must be the earth leader they called

Martin Luther King. I moved closer to the car. I ducked as a rock *whizzed* pass me, cracking a nearby car windshield. The police closed around King. *"Go back to Selma. We don't want you here!"*

The white residents screamed as they overturned cars. King and his entourage defiantly walked to the front of the march and locked arms. A well-aimed rock struck him in the temple. I was right at the back of him. I heard him moan as the impact of the rock slammed against his skull. The blow knocked him to his knees. His trusted comrade, Al, and a police officer helped him up. He staggered as he kept on marching. The marchers started to sing.

"We shall overcome some day!"

The white crowd roared with disapproved shouting *"Nigger go home"* and *"We hate Martin Luther Coon!"*

I gazed at a placard that read: *"King would look good with a knife in his back!"*

I was amazed that despite the violence, hatred, broken noses, gashed skulls, and a river of blood flowing to the streets from their wounds, I did not see one marcher retaliate with violence. I only regret that King's non-violence was not a constant in the universe. The only hope I saw was that the whites that marched with King seemed unwavering in overcoming hatred.

I have traveled to many carbon-based planets, but I have never seen, even in the war-like Cassiopeia galaxy, aliens as hostile as this over skin color as these humans were.

Suddenly, I felt dizzy and hot. I walked away from the march and staggered east when I stumbled and fell on the side of the street. The hot August Chicago heat, without my *frills* regulating my temperature, was weakening me.

A police car pulled up. The same two cops had helped me.

They picked me up and put me in the police car.

"So we meet again," the black cop said sarcastically as he turned around in the front passenger seat, "Too much beer at the March buddy?" The white cop laughed.

"No it's the heat. It's suffocating. But I am okay. Can you drop me off anywhere east?" My tendrils sensed *sahahli* - water - east.

At that moment, a robotic-like voice echoed from a small metallic box up front. "Patrol 12, proceed to 47th and Indiana Avenue ASAP. Be advised a prostitute is fighting with a John. Proceed with caution..."

The white cop pressed a tiny orange button and said, "Patrol 12, read you loud and clear...over!"

I said nothing to them about the many questions that bounced around my skull. I was still wallowing in a sense of relief mingled with bliss that they had saved me from possible death. The pain had vanished from my synthetic body. I felt very much at ease in the patrol car and away from the blistering hot late afternoon. I smiled inwardly as I thought: *I have only been on earth two hours and I have been bombarded with obstacles that I would never have dreamed of happening.* I glanced out of the window as the car sped east. I saw thousands of other cars that operated on the same energy conversion principle. I wondered how long it would take earth science to discover that there was enough energy in a single atom to energize a thousand cars.

Rain started to fall; droplets started to cling to the car's windowpane. I rubbed my sore nose. I sensed that despite the earth's archaic technology they were a very aggressive species. I felt a moment of blinding panic as the car suddenly swerved in front of a woman pointing a knife at a man's throat. The knife gleamed as the car's lights shone on it.

I jerked about in the back seat nervously as the two cops pulled out their guns while leaping out of the car, shouting at the woman, "Alright drop the knife ...now!, Put your hands behind your back and both of you, walk over to the car and put both hands on the door, and stretch your legs...wide!"

A slice of moon dangled over the dilapidated tenement buildings. About 50 black beings gathered around the scene. I got out of the car. My tendrils shook; I felt trouble in the air, the way one feels when a cosmic dust storm is moving toward a starship. But I had no idea what it was. My tendrils detected uncertain vibrations of impending cataclysm. Then suddenly, the black cop stood up, holding 20 small aluminum packages, which glowed in the palm of his hand.

"Dave, looks like we've captured us a pusher man!" he said. "I mean, this guy has got enough heroin to satisfy 100 dope fiends!"

The short, stocky black man looked at the heroin in the cop's hand and turned around, pointing at a woman. He looked wild; eyes glaring in fear, lips drawn back, breathing heavy. Bright globules of sweat, I saw with clarity, covered his black skin. He said in a fearful choking voice, "That dope was planted on me, man. Let me explain. I swear that bitch put it in my pocket!"

He reached down into his waist belt and pulled out a shiny metallic gun pointed it at the small woman. It shook as he shouted, "Didn't you bitch?"

The two cops quickly pulled out their guns.

"Alright mister, put it away! We don't want to kill yah'...now put it down!"

The woman screamed. "What are yah' talking about? I didn't put that dope on you, man. I just want my fuckin' money, niggah!"

Niggah? I wondered why she would call a member of her own race a seemingly degenerate word. Her voice rose to a piercing shriek. "I want my money, niggah!"

The man fired the gun at her three times. The shots echoed through the tall buildings. She ran behind the two cops as blood gushed from her chest. I gasped as six gunshots tore into the man's body. The impact of the bullets seemed to literally pick him up each time one entered his body. The street turned carmine red. The crowd watched his blood-spattered body as it shook spasmodically on the ground; I peered down at the dead man's body on the pavement. As light spilled from a nearby tenement window, I saw a key chain on the body with a stiletto knife on it. There was a neat wad of $100 bills in $20s and $50s. There was a brown wallet; there was a broken syringe with dry, crusted bloodstains on it. His eyes were open. A zigzag of dark blood rolled down his cheek. I was terrified.

The Color of My Blood

The two cops stood next to me looking down at the dead man; they stood beside me, beaming with their power, proud of themselves, swollen with joy. I felt nauseated. I turned and started walking south on Indiana Avenue. I looked back as an ambulance stopped in front of the crowd. I felt in that chaotic instant like fleeing earth and never returning. In only two hours, I perceived earthmen as one of the most barbaric species in the universe.

CHAPTER TWO

I turned east on 48th and Indiana. My eyes nervously scanned the dark, gloomy streets and alleys ahead. I looked in all directions, when suddenly the moon's bright beams cast light on a small four-legged, black furry creature. It growled at me as it scuttled into an alley I approached. My tendrils sensed that the small animal was still lurking behind a large can searching for food. As I passed the alley, the sprawling shadow of the creature reappeared. I gazed at the creature as its beady, fear-ridden eyes looked at me while it snarled viciously. I knew instinctively that the creature was carnivorous. Its fangs glistened from the rays of a nearby street light. It started to snap at me as it made a strange, cough-like sound.

"ARRRF...ARFFF...ERRRRRRRR..ARF..ARF......ERRRRRRRRR.....ARFFFFF...ARF FF.....ERRRR!"

As I mentioned, I still possess some of my alien survival powers. I would never travel to a seemingly barbaric planet without anything to protect myself; but I refuse to use those powers, except when there is no other choice. I have the power of telekinesis. I can move any form of physical matter that weighs less than a ton. Now I could have easily picked up the small creature and hurled it into a building, but why? I could detect that the creature was more frightened than anything else because I represented a scent that was entirely foreign to its olfactory memory bank. I cautiously stepped forward, but the small creature became more confident and started to snap at my leg. I stopped and peered at the creature. I was starting to lose my patience when I saw a short being's shadow as it traversed the alley from the rear of a large tenement building.

"Here TJ, come here TJ, here boy! Good dog, come here boy."

A harsh wind cut through the litter from the streets and sent it whirling into my face. I watched the small black woman as she walked toward the dog and me. Dog? Yes, that's what she called the small beast. Excitement built in me as the woman walked closer. She was short and stout, with small brown almond eyes, black with strands of red braids and a large ass, which conspicuously protruded from her coat. She looked about 25 earth years in age, but I detected a genuine warmness about her and a keen intelligence. When she was about three meters from me, the dog quickly turned around toward her, but still craned its neck, barking nervously at me while scampering toward her at the same time.

It seems that of all the planets, I have traveled to, the F-type and the OM star systems produce the most sensuous females.

The woman knelt down and rubbed the dog on its head, then said to me, "I'm sorry about TJ. He's a little bit nervous of strangers at times, especially at night. That's why I call him TJ because he acts like he's drunk all the time and he also likes wine."

I stood there. I have never felt such unabashed lust before. I wanted that earth woman more than anything. Anything!

"You must be new around here. I don't remember seeing your face - you see, I was born and raised in this neighborhood. I have been living in this building for two years now. I moved in here when I divorced my husband Harold...jeeesus.., it's hot as a bitch's momma out here!" She said while looking at me curiously.

I searched her face for signs of curiosity about me. There was none. I said to her, "My name is Damon James and I am looking for an apartment in this area. Can you help me at all, Miss...?"

"Shirl...Shirl Anderson."

"It's Miss Shirl Anderson then!"

"Mr. Damon James...it's awful hot, would you like to come inside a minute? There might be a vacancy in my building. I have some cold beer to cool you down, Mr. James." She laughed and said, "That's a real unique name... Damon James, it has a ring to it. In fact, there is a Saturday morning cartoon show called *DammonyJames*. My son watches it over at my grandmother's house. Well, would you like to come inside and cool off a bit?"

Her dark brown eyes were hypnotic as I looked at my reflection dance in her orbs. Her hot body trembled.

"I would like to cool off and taste that beer you mentioned, Miss Anderson."

"Damon, forget the formalities, just call me Shirl."

As we neared her building, I ducked under a clothesline. I passed garbage cans and the stench assailed my nostrils.

We walked up a flight of stairs and walked into her small apartment. The small kitchen had shiny flower-print and a torn linoleum on the floor, with a clean yellowish sink, a child's rocking chair, a large bag of dog food, and an assortment of kitchen appliances.

I wondered as I sat down in her kitchen chair why she would randomly invite a strange man into her living quarters. I soon found out why.

"Damon, ah, you do know what I'm about, don't you? I mean, I didn't just think you wanted cold beer, eh?"

I looked at her with astonishment as she walked out of her bedroom with a pink negligee on. I could see her nude body very clearly. My three hearts banged and banged and banged.

"*About*, Shirl?"

"Right, I mean, you're no idiot. I mean you do know what I'm *about?*"

"Well, Shirl, you have to excuse my ignorance. What exactly do you mean 'about'?"

"About money. All mighty green, you dig? I could tell outside you wanted some of this pussy. Now you can have me for the right price, which is $25. Rather cheap, don't you think?"

She walked toward me and grabbed my hat. I quickly pulled down on the brim.

"What's wrong, don't you want to get comfortable?"

"Yes, I'll take off my coat, but I have this taboo about taking my hat off even in the summer time. You know, sort of a superstious thing."

"Oh, so you believe in that nonsense, huh?"

"Well, not exactly, it's just something I like to study."

"Well, I always say to each and everybody, do your own thing. Now how yah' like yah' beer in a class or can?"

"Just like yours...please."

"Look, Damon, are you nervous about something? Relax; I am not going to bite cha. Even if you ain't got no money we can still talk. Where are you from anyway?"

As she snapped open the beer can and gave it to me, I gulped it down while thinking: what if she discovered my real identity? But should I even let an obviously simple woman intimidate me, a being that has traversed the stars? Then again, every planet I have traveled to have its own little differences, and so did the beings. Earthlings on average strike me as highly intelligent, despite their primitive technological progress. I was afraid. A multitude of nagging questions bounced within my head. How do earthlings reproduce? I knew the basic structure of the male and female species, but I had no knowledge of how their reproductive organs operated. My synthetic body started trembling with desire.

My Versai penis stiffened into a half-moon with an incredible hardness. TJ started to growl at me as he lay in the corner when I slapped her hands away from my hat .

"Let me show you a good time, Damon," she said, wiggling her curvaceous body in front of me. I fe1t sensuous; flames were jumping in my body. She tempted me. She lured me. I frantically grabbed her large buttocks and started to kiss her small nipples. She squirmed. She moaned. She sighed. I felt ill at ease. My tendrils sensed the woman was in heat

"Shall we have a drink while we discuss money, Mr. James?" I nodded my head as she walked into the bedroom. I heard the crackle of glasses. She walked back out with two glasses full of a light brown liquor. I coughed as I gulped down the hot liquid. Shirl smiled sensuously.

"Damn, man, where you learn to drink like that...you want some more?"

My face flushed purple as the hot liquid engorged my chest with a hot searing, like gas.

"No, no - I assure you, that's quite enough."

The reek of her scent oozed into my nostrils. We smiled at each other under a bulb's yellowish glow. I slipped my arms around her large, round ass.

"Business first, Damon," she said. "Then pleasure!" She held out her hand, indicating she wanted money.

I retain the ability to create what earthlings would call three-dimensional holographic illusions. Any physical object I see I can replicate a holographic illusion of it for 15 minutes. I remembered the money I had seen at the murder scene. I knew instinctively that it was some kind of medium that served as exchange. I knew exactly what it looked like.

We don't use such primitive methods on Untrov because there is no need. Everything on my planet needed for survival is free, plentiful, and readily available.

I glanced at her purse on the table next to my empty liquor glass. I wondered if there was any money in the purse. I knew that there was only one way to find out. I focused my telekinetic power on the purse and made it tumble to the floor. Objects poured out of it: green papers with the numerals five and 10; there were four of them. There were some silver and brown coins, a stiletto knife, a small blue ink pen, a sharp razor, a syringe wrapped in aluminum foil. Finally, I saw a small package wrapped in foil that looked just like the packages the cops had found on the man that I saw get killed.

"Did you see that?" Shirl asked.

"What?" I said nervously.

"The way my purse just damn near jumped off the table...I mean...wow...you didn't see it?"

"No...maybe it is the alcohol. Maybe you're seeing things, Shirl?"

"I tell you I saw that purse just hop up and fall on the floor! It was as though it had a mind of its very own."

She rose from her chair, knelt down to pick up the objects, and put them back in her purse. I focused my replication powers on the money in my mind, and money started to materialize in my inner coat pocket. By the time she had reset the purse back on the table, I held 25 crisp dollar bills in my hand. I only hoped she didn't notice that they were the same denomination as her own money.

She looked at the money and smiled. "Thank you." She snatched the money out of my hand as if I were going to change my mind. "Maybe I better have another drink." She walked back into the bedroom.

I heard the clacking as TJ swaggered into the kitchen growling.

ARKKK...ARFFF...ERR.ARFFF...EERRRR!

I smiled inwardly. I wonder if the dog actually perceived that I was pulling a fast one on Shirl.

Shirl walked back into the kitchen with her drink and screamed at the dog. "Now shut up! You just shut up and take your ass in the front room. Now git! Git! Go! Git!"

The dog eyed me viciously as it strode across the wooden floor and back into the front room. It flattered my ego that I alone had powers that earthlings never dreamed of (even though my tendrils detected a quantum of psi powers).

Excitement built in me as I glanced at her very large, very soft ass. For some unfathomable reason I liked the feel of the earthling female's soft flesh. It reminded me of the Magnoi female on Magno; a star system only five light years from my planet, Untroz. The Magnoi females were built similar to the earth women. The main difference was the limbs: the Magnoi females had a sort of octopus thorax with three arms on each side, and their legs were devoid of ossified bone, which made them very pliable and capable of almost acrobatic positions. But of all my galactic travels to habitable planets, earth females seemed to be the most sensuous.

Shirl put her lips to my ear. "Let's fuck," she murmured. "I have such a strange urge about your vibes. And believe me, I've been through many men. But you seem so very different, I almost feel weak with desire, and what's so absurd about all this is that I'm a prostitute. I'm normally very businesslike, but you seem so strange....Enuf words - let's fuck!"

I started to sweat. As I stood up my half-moon shaped stiff penis hurt, it was so hard. I had to crouch so the upper portion of my body would coordinate with the angle of my penis, which would hopefully alleviate the pain.

We stepped into her bedroom. It was very sparse, with only a large bed in the center of it and an old chair sat adjacent. A red light hovered over the bed. The smell of incense engulfed the room. She walked out into the bathroom, slamming the door behind her. I quickly undressed and folded my clothes neatly on the chair. I walked over to the mirror and gazed at my sweaty synthetic body. I smiled as I thought about how authentic it looked. It was flawless; at least externally. I wondered how I was going to prevent her from hearing my three hearts banging.

In a subconscious way, Shirl frightened me. Not because she might discover my real identity, but because she reminded me, so much of Charloi, the bitch in the Beta Grevatoi Star System, who stumped and crushed my three throbbing hearts. The pain from her evil ways still cling to me.

Shirl walked back into the room and closed the door. I heard TJ scratching on the door. She walked toward her dresser, picked up a short, thin, brown-colored stick, and tossed it to me.

"What is this?" I asked, confused.

"Damon, are you serious?"

"Yes, very...now what is this; some sort of herbal medicinal drug?"

"Look, you sure you from this planet, man? Like *that* my good man is a joint - cannabis? You dig. Or marijuana... Mary Jane...that's the best. its *boe*...go on, fire it up!" She walked over to me and we sat down on the bed. She snatched the stick from me and said, "Dig, Damon, now you listen closely...you take the joint and you hold it in your mouth like this." I watched her as she held the joint in her mouth. "Then you kind of pucker your lips, then you light it, like so, then you inhale it. Take long drags...*siiish...siiich...sitccccosh!*"

She handed me the joint. I slowly put it between my lips. I inhaled, inhaled, and inhaled, then started coughing and coughing. I balled up like a fetus while coughing. I held onto my hat as my body contorted into a knot.

Shirl parted her lips to speak. "Wow! Say, you all right, Damon? I'll get you some water." She ran back into the kitchen and rushed back to the bedroom, handing me the glass of water. I quickly gulped it down.

"Thanks, I feel a lot better. Please put that out, even the fumes disturb me." She reached over me and squashed the joint out in a patterned glass bowl.

A draught of air blasted forward from a crevice in the window. The night breeze swept impetuously over the bedroom, stirring the curtains. I shivered with nausea. The joint had somehow momentarily dazed the inner workings of my synthetic body. I could feel the circuitry fighting off the foreign fumes inside me.

She stood and grabbed me around the neck, rubbing my cheeks. I gazed up at her eyes; the blind lust seemed to lock on my stare. I detected something strange going on. I don't know, maybe it was the joint, but I felt something unusual on the verge of happening.

She tossed her negligee to the floor. She was completely nude. I stood and she grabbed me around the waist. My stiff penis stuck her in the stomach because she was so much smaller than I was.

"Damn Damon, God sure was generous with you!" she said as she tried to put her small hand around it. "I ain't never seen a dick shaped like a half moon."

She tiptoed on her feet and her moist, taut lips brushed against mine. I maneuvered her near the bed. I was nervous.

A multitude of questions bounced around my skull. How do I do it? Is it just a question of entering her being? Is penetration the key? But my tendrils detected that she wanted me to dominate her. She let go of my dick and tumbled onto the bed. She jackknifed her legs. I peered at a hairy, v-shaped organ. I saw a dark orifice that lurked beneath the hair. I quickly gazed down at my stiff penis. It was only logical that...why, that was it! So simple and yet so complex! I walked over to her gaping legs. My penis throbbed. I knew now exactly what to do. My three hearts felt as though they were going to tear out of my chest.

She bellowed out, "Fuck me, Damon! Fuck me good!"

Her hand reached for mine unwittingly. I rubbed her ass. She shuddered. Globules of sweat formed on her face. Her mouth snarled. Her pupils dilated. Her nostrils flared. Her skin flushed. It was as though she had metamorphosed into an entirely different specie.

My mind shifted for a brief micro second. I thought about all my vast voyages to other worlds. I have fought the Laxor people in Alpha Betro IV. I have taught the Zuni people in the dry crystal blue desert of Petra VIII. I have been marooned on Jupiter amid the millions of primeval beasts. I have made love to the strange Magnoi females in the Beta Gravatai Star System; were females who are known for their powers to kill aliens with their sexual traps. And now, I peer down at an earth woman whose eyes are like two marble stones found in a Venusian cave.

I snapped back to reality as Shirl pulled on my waist. I started to tremble as I lowered by body. Shirl grabbed my penis and guided me. My mind became a churning mass of brain parts pulsating with incredible energy. Then I heard...I remembered...it was Trevil, the chief scientist lecturing me before I departed Untroz:

> *"Scribe, your duty is to record all of the ethnic cultural behaviorist patterns of earth's culture. Remember, no inter-species sex, Scribe. Remember: the earthling species is different. They are different in kind...and degree. Remember your mission, Scribe: record, observe, watch, and understand. But no biological mingling. I repeat, Scribe, no sex, Scribe. None. I repeat no interspecies sex, Scribe. None - I repeat..."*

"Come on, what yah' waiting for, fah' christsake? Put it in...c'mon!"

In a rage, I thought, *just one time won't hurt. The universe won't go big bang if I...I..*I withdrew murmuring, "I can't, Shirl...I just can't!"

Shirl looked at me, her brown eyes beamed anger, her face snarled, seething with animal lust. Her eyes were pleading. "You what?"

"I...I can't!"

The Color of My Blood

She was furious. Then before I could do anything, she grabbed my penis and thrust it inside her. I bit my lower lip for I knew it was too late. I thought, *I'm sorry Trevil, but you probably would do the same thing.* Blotches of sweat formed on her tiny pug nose. She pushed my phallus farther and farther within her hairy orifice. Her eyes widened. Her jaw sagged. Drools of saliva dripped from the corners of her mouth.

I parted my mouth to scream. She quickly covered my mouth with her hand. I had lost control. I could see Trevil's face grimacing with anger because he knew that only during the sex act do we transform into our true selves. I glanced at my hands; they were turning, changing, transforming into nonhuman reptilian-like claws. She knocked off my hat. I knew then it was too late. Her eyes were closed and I knew that when she opened them and looked at those snake-like tendrils writhing on my head, she would probably faint.

I realized that it was too late to worry, so I concentrated all of my energy on making love to her in a way no earth woman had ever experienced: A geyser of oily secretions started to form all over my body. I was slowly changing into my Versai-real body. I started to exude an acrid odor that smelled like perfume. It tingled her nostrils.

Her eyes were still closed as she mumbled, "Good, Damon...so very gooood!" She laid even farther back and jackknifed her legs into a missionary position.

My penis started to sprout cilia-like moving hairs on its tip, which rubbed the inside of her orifice. I glanced at my body. I had changed into a large reptilian scaly creature. Seventy percent of my body had changed. I expulsed a blue fume-like gaseous odor from my body, so that when she did open her eyes she could not see my changed anatomy, at least I thought.

She started to cough uncontrollably. The bedroom slowly became enveloped in the gaseous fumes. She opened her eyes. Suddenly she screamed. "My GAWD!" One of my long tentacles extended from my back and curled around her mouth like an infuriated snake. Blind fear shot through her being. The tentacle unleashed an aphrodisiac fume into her nostrils, then it released her and she screamed again. "Ohhhh Gawd, what are you?"

"I'm from the planet Untroz, Shirl. But I'm still a male. You see, Shirl, some things never change. Even in the outer regions of the universe, sex is a primal urge...but you must not be fearful. You're going to enjoy this experience. Just think; this is history...two different species copulating. You're the first earth female," I started to laugh, "I have ever...you know..."

She smiled and relaxed. I knew the aphrodisiac was working. The warmness of her body made me forget, momentarily, that she was human.

- ◊ -

As I looked at Damon, I trembled with fear; spectral lust exuded from his hypnotic-like gaze. He then started to squint. His eyes were snake-like; a bright yellow orb with a black vertical strip down the middle, his once handsome ebony face started to transform into a dragon or a lizard before my very eyes. I felt like vomiting. He started mumbling.

OH, EARTHLING. I'M ONLY GOOD FOR 20 OF YOUR MINUTES. OH...OH - COPULATE, HURRY...LORD!

I trembled as long greenish tendrils started to burst out of his changing body. I shuddered as Damon morphed into a clammy, hairy, dark nauseous green reptilian male. He was horrific looking.

GOD SHIRL...COPULATE!

I closed my eyes. It was a nightmare. But he was the best lay I had ever had. It was only the looking at him that disturbed me. I listened as Damon mumbled.

"The sexual cycle in you humans and other lower life forms is radically inferior to ours. The male in our species is only satisfied, or as you earthlings say, have an orgasm, only when we copulate with a different species like you and I...you see, we aren't supposed to have sex with other aliens...and yet that is the only true time we can enjoy the act. I am...am...ohhh it's so gooood...oh sweet divine force...ohhhh mighty RAFBAC!"

I started panting with excitement as a tiny finger rubbed on my spine and genitals. I peered at Damon's face; it was normal again. I glanced at the lower portion of his body. It was still lizard like. Suddenly I felt thousands of nerve fibers on his belly scratching sensuously on my stomach. A jelly-like secretion oozed out of the tiny nerve fibers. I had never felt such warmth and lust.

Damon spoke to me again telepathically, "My telepathic sensors will make me your dream man. Remember Sweetback Sam, Shirl?"

I thought, yes indeed, that was some man. I hate to think about him. He was absolutely fantastic! Oh, before I could bat an eye, I gazed up at Sweetback Sam's sweaty muscular body humping on top of me. I screamed, "Oh, Sweetback, that's so good. I mean, it's really you?" My body wanted to burst with pleasure.

"Yeah, baby, it's me...long stroke Sam..." He plunged harder.

"Yes, indeed, it's you. You still got the best dick in the world. Oh Jeesus, it's so good!"

"Ain't it...um...um...JEEEEESUS!"

I closed my eyes as his manhood surged out of his being. Sweetback then transformed back into the clammy lizard like creature and said,

"For you lower life forms these specialized hallucinogenic receptor cells of the body are used for gaining information about experience and your environment..."

I screamed out with orgiastic bliss. "its sooo good...it's...so...so good...umm!" I was having a flurry of orgasms. It was incredible, unreal, a dream. I screamed,

"I'm...commmming....gawd!"

"The sensations you are experiencing are created by my telepathic sensors. I know what Sweetback Sam was like: Each of my telepathic sensors sends impulses to a particular part of your brain; orgasm receptors send impulses to orgasm centers in the brain, memory receptors send impulses to memory centers, and so on. Thought, pain, lust, joy, sadness...all can exist if I monitor the right impulse centers. I even know what type of sexual olfactory receptor to tap."

A gush of strong, sexual odor tickled my nostrils. At that point, a low frequency hum stimulated my ear. It was a sensuous hum. It was the moan of Sweetback Sam. Then suddenly Damon, in his alien body, scuttled over me and scooted off the bed. He looked like a large, hairy man-like reptile,...I watched him as he transformed back into his earth body. He quickly put on his clothes. I lay in bed, too weak to move.

He gazed at me and said, "How do you feel, Shirl?"

"Just wonderful, I mean, I have never felt so fulfilled." Then I rolled over on my stomach and thought, *It must have been the weed* and I went to sleep.

- ◊ -

My sensors detected that earth was on the brink of another ice age. I started to walk out of Shirl's apartment today and I almost fainted from the scorching heat. I mean, the temperature was in the 90s. I glanced at a Sunday *Chicago Tribune* newspaper headline on the vestibule floor: **THE COMING ICE AGE**. I quickly picked up the paper and discovered some interesting facts that attested to the astonishing accuracy of Trevil's prophetic vision. I read that Chicago was in the midst of its hottest summer. When I first arrived on earth my tendrils sensed that the planet was undergoing some major climatic changes. I detected that earth was experiencing a major cooling period. The only thing preventing the onslaught of a major ice age was the amount of carbon dioxide in the atmosphere, which ironically enough warms the earth's atmosphere, thereby forestalling the coming ice age.

Trevil had told me that earth had changed dramatically since his great,

great, great grandfather's last visit. He said that North America and Africa separated 200 million years ago. Trevil has drawings that his great grandfather made from 400 miles up that clearly verify that Africa and Arabia were once one.

RELATIVE SIZE UNTROZ AND EARTH

	UNTROZ	EARTH
Equator Diameter (Earth=7,926m)	12.6	1
Mass	319.1	1
Volume	1319	1
Density (water)	4.02	5.52
Equatorial Surface Gravity	3.31	1
Number of Satellites	8	1
Rotation on Axis	16 hours	1 day
Revolution Around Sun	13.80 years	1 year
Mean Dist. From Sun or Teli	80,000,000m	91,956,524m

CHAPTER THREE

Shirl helped me to get a small apartment in her building. I was pleased that it was on the opposite side of her building. You see, there were two entrances to the building, so in order for Shirl to visit me she must physically leave her building. Now do not get me wrong, I like Shirl; but ever since our little sexual excursion, I cannot have any peace. She has turned into a sex-crazed female.

My apartment was almost identical to Shirl's, except that mine was in the rear and I had to walk out of my apartment to get to my kitchen and washroom. At night, I could hear almost every sound in the building: The sensuous screams of a woman fucking; the tick-toc-tic of my clock over my mirror; the gnawing *tap-tap* of a leaky water faucet in the kitchen; the clank of my radiator as it started to heat; even rodents fighting in the washroom. Most humans would be rather perturbed that they had to leave their apartment to use the washroom and kitchen, but it really didn't bother me because I don't eat or excrete waste materials like humans. I'm glad I don't because it's such a cumbersome act.

I had been creating a lot of illusory money to buy certain contraptions that fascinated me. Yesterday I went out and bought a stereo receiver, two speakers, a turntable, and many Jazz albums...or is it Dazz? I was thinking about going out today to buy some Coltrane, Cecil Taylor, Ornett Coleman, Holtz, Mozart, Eric Dorphy, Sunra, Lateef, Shostakovich, Davis, ,Mingus, Bird, and endless others that I hadn't bought. But I stayed in and listened to *Peace Piece* by Bill Evans over and over again. Evan's piano voicing remind that there must exist some kind of creative-harmonic-convergence in the universe for all life forms. I was seriously thinking about kidnapping him and taking him back to Untroz to let Trevil check him out.

When you considered that sound is merely a series of compressions and refractions of air that travel considerably slower than light — about 331 meters per second, but fast nevertheless — it's absolutely astonishing how a Jazz musician via improvisation, can make decisions at velocities that are uncanny, yet the results are breath taking beautiful creations.

I often wondered why earth scientists have not investigated this phenomenon. It possibly could add in solving the unified field theory that unify space-time-matter and energy. I had been reading everything I could get my claws on... my hands on...because of the heat wave in my apartment. I bought hundreds of books on this sound phenomena earthlings call Jazz. I thought it would be far more appropriate to call it audio-kinetic-creative-energy. I recently stumbled across a passage that touched some ideas that are similar to mine:

Jazz is the deep plunge into the creative abyss.

Jazz represents the transcendence of spirit over matter.

Jazz is the fusion of the mind/body synthesis.

From my readings of Jazz, I thought that earth scholars should re-evaluate it and consider it as one of the major modern contributions to world history. I thought the Jazz artist, through intuition, perceive galactic truths and unknowingly express them through his instrument. I also felt that the instruments these artists used were archaic. The instruments' architectonic structure hampered the artist from using the whole spectrum of his sensibilities. In fact, when you consider that the human being can speak at only a maximum of 150 words per minute, which creates a separateness, then you can understand how limited the great Jazz musician is with his artificial means of communication. What they need is an instrument that can reproduce every quantum of their purgation of creativity...an instrument that eliminates any wasted time-lapse between bodies and instrument..

I had listened to quite a lot of John Coltrane. His music reminded me of the Frenoi people in the Alpha Unac Star System who have succeeded in using sound as an energy source. At any rate, Trane attempted, through sound, to de-solidify, to break matter into quantum, by shifting and radically experimenting with sheets-of- sound energy. Trane changed the way sound energy notations reach human ears, for sound is energy.

TAP, TAP...TAP...TAP, TAP!

My door. I wondered who it could be. "Who is it?"

The Color of My Blood

"James, it's me, Aaron. Say, there are some dudes at the front door that want to see you. They look like cops to me. Anything wrong?"

"No! I'll be right there. Thanks, Aaron!"

I said *no* with concern because, since I had moved into the building, I noticed that Aaron's door screeched open every night at 12 and closed at 3 a.m. One morning I noticed bloody footprints and blotches of dried blood near his door.

I quickly put up my notes and was walking down my gloomy hallway toward the vestibule when suddenly two large rats scampered out of the bathroom, fighting. Their eyes glistened in the retracted light of the hallway. They snarled and screeched and fought ferociously, totally unaware of my presence. I stepped forward and the rats stopped fighting and stared at me. The hair on their backs arched as their glistening fangs snapped. They scuttled back into the washroom.

I hurriedly walked toward the front door. I noticed a strange look in the men's eyes. It was the same demented look I had seen when those two cops gunned down that man. I listened to the muted sound of street traffic. I was nervous. Tension crackled in the air. I stood in the doorway for a moment, and then nervously grabbed the doorknob as the white man flashed a badge on me.

The black cop banged his fist on the door's window. I opened the door. The tendrils beneath my hat writhed with nervousness.

"Hello!" I said, confused.

"Why so nervous?" the white cop asked.

I looked away from his eyes, trying to hide my fear.

"Well?" he said impatiently,

"Well, what?"

"Look, Mr. James, don't play the nut-role, okay...a woman was murdered and raped in the building last night."

"What? You mean..."

"We mean just that. She was stabbed 50 times with a butcher knife. By the way, I'm Detective Milton Olerhy, and this is my partner Detective Joe 'Tank' Morgan. The black detective nodded his head. Olerhy cleared his throat and continued. "Damon James, that is your name, isn't it?"

"Yes, it is."

"According to the Supreme Court decision of 1966 in the case of Miranda versus Arizona, I must advise you of your rights, so listen up."

"But...you don't think that I—"

"That's beside the point, Mr. James. You have the right to remain silent; if you choose, you do not have to answer any questions. In addition, if you do answer any questions, they may be used as evidence against you."

I nodded my head nervously. My tendrils twitched and writhed under my hat.

"You have the right to consult with an attorney before or after questioning. And, if you desire counsel but can't afford it, we will have a lawyer appointed without cost, so you can consult with him during and after questioning. You comprehend all that, Mr. James?"

"Yes, but I haven't done anything..."

"Do you want a lawyer, Mr. James?"

"No...for what?"

"Mr. James, we are investigating a rape-murder. A woman that lived in this building was raped and murdered. It was the work of a very, very sick man. The victim's name is Shirl Anderson. You know her?"

"Sure I know her...but - you mean she is dead?"

"Is Seven-Up, Mr. James?" the black cop said slyly.

"Why would anyone want to kill Shirl? I mean...I just can't believe someone would want to kill her. Why, I just saw her yesterday."

Detective Olerhy cleared his throat. "Maybe because of money, sex, dope...it could be ad infinitum of reasons. We do know that Shirl kept a very up-to-date diary, that's why we knew your name and address. We're checking out every John that she dealt with; so help make our job easier by cooperating Mr. James, huh?"

"I didn't murder her!" I said frantically.

"Just be cool," the black cop said as he patted me on the shoulder condescendingly. "Why were you so nervous at the door, James?"

"Look," I said, trying to reason with them, "I didn't murder her. I really liked her. But cops make me nervous, you know. Last week I saw two cops gun down a man. Ever since then I've been a little nervous ...but I tell you I didn't kill her! Why would I? Besides, she always treated me fairly!"

"Look, Mr. James, all we want is some information from yah...we aren't stupid; we don't have a yellow sheet on yah. You ain't got ah record. Just be straight with us. Now..." The white cop said.

My mind became a whirling, churning machine producing thousands of images of Shirl; Shirl smiling; Shirl sad; Shirl frowning; Shirl angry; Shirl happy; Shirl sensuous; Shirl dead!

"Ah...Mr. James?"

"Yes...I didn't mean to drift off on you, but this is just really unbelievable."

"That's where you're wrong. It's very real, Mr. James. We want you to come down to headquarters for questioning. Don't get frantic, Mr. James, we know where you were last night. In fact, one of your neighbors called the desk complaining about loud Jazz music coming from your apartment."

The light in the hallway popped on. I glanced at our shadows as they danced on the walls.

"We have suspects and we want to know if you have seen any in the area before," Detective Olerhy said.

"Mr. James, we will be waiting in the car!" I was numb, shocked, bewildered. I balled my fists nervously.

"Sure, anything I can do. I'll just lock my door."

As they walked out of the building, I sensed the loss of Shirl. I felt weak and nauseated. I walked down my dark hallway visualizing Shirl's dismembered body sprawled on the floor: Her once pretty ebony face cold and ashy; her glassy eyes and fleshy lips dry and blurred by death; her shapely figure sliced like a butcher's carcass; her bed overflowing with a river of carmine blood. The thought of death was not something that I dwelled on back home, but here on earth it seemed to permeate every facet of one's being. I found myself trembling as I walked into the room. My three hearts beat with hard tension. I wanted to scream. Earth is such a vicious and rotten fuckin' planet. I grabbed a shirt and locked my door, and started walking down my long dark hallway toward the front door and to the police car.

CHAPTER FOUR

"Chief McNeil, this is Mr. Damon James."

I looked at the short, stocky white man with silver hair and a menacing smile. He stretched out his hand. "Mr. James, this is Joseph Shapiro, our medical examiner."

The ME was a short, queasy Italian with bulbous, owl-like eyes that seemed to pop out of their sockets as he said, "Shirl Anderson was butchered by an authentic nut. I mean, in all my 20 years in the business, I have never seen a body dismembered like this. He cut up the mammary glands, the carotid, trachea, the jugular, the stomach... it's just sickening!"

The ME was the kind of guy that made you feel like something slimy was on you. I noticed as he was talking that Chief McNeil unconsciously started scratching his arms. He acted as though spiders were crawling on him. I watched the ME as he wiped his forehead with a clean white handkerchief.

Then he frowned and said, "And to add to this grotesque nightmare, you wouldn't believe what the coroner's tentative necropsy report has discovered...Chief, can I use your phone?"

"Sure...go right ahead."

The ME trembled as he picked up the phone, dialed, "Alright, Mac, are you ready down there? Okay we will be right down...give us five minutes, eh?"

He slammed down the phone, "Gentlemen, we are going downstairs to the mortuary...you must see this with your own eyes."

The ME opened the door as myself, Detective Olerhy, Jones, and Chief McNeil walked out of the office and entered the elevator.

As we crammed into it, the chief coughed and cleared his throat then said, "At this point, Mr. James, we have put out a 10-69 to the patrol cars in the area of the rape-murder. This is very serious; this maniac is a very sick man. I don't know if Detective Olerhy and Jones have mentioned this, but this is the sixth victim this month, in six different locations: Bronzeville, Hyde Park, Englewood, and as far south as Grand Crossing. At best we are speculating that it is the same rapist because all the victims were prostitutes and butchered just like Shirl. At this point any suspicious male or known rapist in the vicinity of 4852 South Prairie Avenue, and presumably heading south toward 55th and Washington Park, will be approached for the slightest probably cause." The chief sighed and lit a cigarette, coughed, and continued,

"We already have suspects...that's why we brought you down here for the lineup. At this point, we are assuming it was a rape-murder, but when the necropsy report comes in we'll be positively sure. We know without a shadow of a doubt that we are dealing with a sadistic murderer."

The elevator door quickly opened. A large white sign loomed into view.

MORGUE

DR. JOSEPH SHAPIRO
COOK COUNTY MEDICAL EXAMINER
ONLY IDENTIFIED PERSONNEL
ALLOWED INSIDE

I glanced around the large antiseptic room. Bright fluorescent lights cast ominous shadows on the walls. An alcoholic dampness pervaded the room. I bumped into a gurney with a body on it that was angled against the corridor wall. The sheet fell from the head of the corpse. I nervously looked at the head of a young black male around 22 years old. I gazed closer. I felt nauseous. The top of his head had been blown away. Grey noodle like strands hung out. I looked at his arm; a four-cornered star tattoo on it said *Black Gangster Disciple*. His dead brown eyes stared defiantly at the ceiling as if it was falling down. His fist was still balled as if in anger; his limp arm hung from the gurney.

A tall, razor-thin white man with purplish, pockmarked skin approached the ME. He looked like the walking dead.

"Mr. Shapiro, everything is ready, sir."

The ME turned toward the morgue attendant and said, "Alright, Mac, pull the body over here and turn on some more lights....Jeeesus, how can you see in here?"

The Color of My Blood

After turning on the lights the attendant pushed the body on a three-wheel cart in front of us. The reek of death was intense, concentrated, pervading the whole room. The cool white fluorescent light lit up the morgue and cast eerie shadows on the white sheet, which covered Shirl's body that lay before us. I fought a swelling nausea as the attendant glanced at the ME waiting for him to nod his head so we could gaze at her stiff corpse.

The ME said, "Gentlemen, what you are on the verge of seeing must be kept in utmost secrecy. At this point only eight people will have seen this: myself, Detective Olerhy, Detective Jones, Mr. James, Chief McNeil, the coroner and Mack, the morgue attendant. We are reluctant to divulge any information about this bizarre crime until we are certain that the capture of this fanatic is close at hand. Alright, Mack."

Mack slowly pulled back the sheet. I knew it was Shirl, despite her shrunken cheeks and patchy hair. Her eyes were open, glassy, fixed, frightened. It was as though she had seen something horrible before she died. Her lips were drawn back in excruciating pain. Her trachea and stern mastoid were cut in half. There were bloodstains all over her head. I noticed a thin glistening oily-like secretion that seemed to cover her entire head.

, "Why is she so oily?" the chief bellowed out," I mean, normally after rigor mortis sets in they are as dry and as cold as ice. It looks like she has been dipped into some sort of slime. Mack, has anyone been tampering with this body?"

"No one, chief, but to be honest with you sometimes I do hear a strange noise coming from inside her. Sounds sort of like the squirming of a cat. Could just be my imagination though."

"Chief," the ME said as he wiped his forehead with his handkerchief, "you haven't seen nothing yet." He nodded his head to the attendant, who pulled down the sheet past her mammary glands.

"Oh, Gawd, who could do such a thing?" Detective Jones said nervously.

We looked at two gaping incisions that took the place of her mammary glands.

"Alright, let's just get on with this. I don't have all night. What exactly do you want us to see?" The chief hollered.

"Alright, Mack," the ME said. "Pull the sheet all the way off!"

I nervously glanced at her bloated stomach. The chief scratched his head.

"What in the hell is that protruding out of her stomach....is she pregnant?" he asked nervously.

"Uh, uh, chief," the ME said. "I wish it was that simple. Chief, take a good close look at her stomach and you'll see what I mean."

Chief McNeil leaned over the corpse and strained his eyes looking at the bulge on her knife-slashed stomach. Suddenly it rippled. Fearfully, the chief jumped back from it.

"Jeeeesus, did you see that? It...it moved. You mean, Shapiro, after 50 brutal stabs with a butcher knife, the baby or whatever it is, is still alive? I can't believe it...holy Christ!"

"Chief, you said baby, but we don't know what it is inside her. In fact, it won't register under X-rays or ultrasounds. It's something that is beyond our definition of living life..."

"You mean..." the chief started to sweat as he lit another cigarette, "that it's something we don't even know about?"

"I mean just that", the ME pressed down on her stomach it's hard as a rock! Eventually we are going to call in some specialist, but we just don't have the answers, Chief."

My tendrils started writhing, coiling, and quivering. I sensed what we were gazing at. I knew what Shirl Anderson was serving as a host for: *My child!*

"It looks like a cocoon for a butterfly or something," Mack said fearfully.

"Look, it's coming out of her!" Detective Olerhy said frantically.

I looked at Shirl's dead body as the larvae-cocoon-like fetus spilled out of her vagina. Shirl's limp, dead body twitched and jerked. I knew it was my offspring. It was a male. Only the male offspring are born in a pink-like-husk. I could hear it communicating with me telepathically.

"Father, I am your child...Father, I detect danger...Father, help me...Father, am I not a product of your seed?...Father, save me...."

, "I'm going to kill it!" The chief shouted as he pulled out his gun.

My three hearts banged frantically. What could I do to save my child? I grabbed the chief by the shoulder. "Chief, wait...that might help us find the killer. Don't kill it, pleasssse!"

"Hogwash!" the Chief screamed out as he pushed me down on the floor. "It's ghastly and it could be some kind of parasite or disease or something!"

"Save me, Father..."

Chief McNeil aimed his Magnum at the writing larvae as its reptilian head started to break out of its shell.

"I detect death, Father, save me...."

Catooom...Catoooo. Click...Catuopom. Click. The Chief fired six rounds at the reptile that had broken through the shell. Green blood oozed from its body.

"Father, I'm dying..."

It was dead. I cradled my head in my hands. My son was dead.

"Mack, burn it up and let's get the hell out of here. This place gives me the creeps. They should be ready for the lineup now anyway." The chief said with disgust.

"But chief," the ME pleaded, "We need to find out what it is. How do we know if her clients have contacted a disease from this thing? How do we know it is not harboring a killer microbe? All it takes is one lethal microbe that is resistant to our antibiotics and we are all doomed!"

"Alright...bag it up and make your test and send it to the CDC authorities!" Chief McNeill said cautiously as he looked at his watch.

"They should be ready for the lineup. Now let's get out of here!"

CHAPTER FIVE

We crammed back into the elevator. I could still hear my son's voice:

"*Father, I'm dying. Father, I'm dying.*" I was full of revulsion and hatred for Chief McNeil, but I understood the *why* of his actions: In his universe, he thought he had done the right thing. I also understood that the child had to be a mutant, purely because of our genetic incompatibility with humans.

The elevator came to a screeching halt on the second floor. The aluminum doors opened silently and our feet sank into a lush blue carpet as we followed the Chief down a long maze of doors. I quickly thought about what I could do to help find Shirl's murderer. We came to an abrupt halt at a door with the words "INVESTIGATIVE LINEUP" written in large, bold white letters. As we entered the room, my eyes immediately glued to a brightly lit stage platform about four meters in front of me. We quickly walked down the aisle of the small auditorium and sat down in the front row. The Chief said, "Alright, Kirk, send them out!"

A beam of light flickered on quickly and the whole stage lit up like a star in nova. Then seven men slowly walked out from behind a large wall: six black and one white. I peered at each one with absolute acuity. Was that Aaron, my neighbor? My tendrils underneath my hat started writhing with absolute panic. I sensed something, and yet I couldn't decipher what it really was. I thought about the dried blood in front of his door. I thought and thought and thought. There was something sick and diabolical about him. I knew Aaron had something to do with Shirl's death. I just didn't have hard evidence. But maybe the dried blood and bloody footprints could be tested for Shirl's DNA?

"Mr. James, do any of them look vaguely familiar?" The chief looked at me as though hoping I would say yes.

"Chief, I would like to view them in profile if you don't mind."

"Sure." He hollered at them, "Alright, gentlemen, let's have a side view...move!"

I looked at each one. I pulled the brim down on my fedora because my tendrils were so active it actually seemed as though my hat was going to pop off any minute.

"Well, Mr. James?" the chief asked inquisitively.

"Aaron, you killed Shirl, didn't you?" I shouted. "Was that Shirl's dried blood near your door? Chief McNeil, I think he killed Shirl and all the other women!"

"You fuckin' lying man! I ain't killed nobody. I tell you he is lying'!"

"Alright," the chief bellowed out angrily. "Put him back in the lockup. The rest of you can go. But don't leave town!" The Chief rose up from his seat . "Mr. James, let's get a cup of coffee in my office."

"Sure, why not?"

As we walked into his office, I quickly glanced out of his window at a scorching Lake Michigan landscape. I sensed that the Chief wanted to ask me questions about Aaron being Shirl's killer, despite the fact that his location at the time of the murder was not documented. He sat down in his swivel chair, snarled with frustration, pressed a small button on this desk, and spoke into his intercom system.

"Mary, send Detective Olerhy and Jones into my office!"

"Will do, Chief."

He cleared his throat and started tapping a pencil nervously on his desk., "Mr. James, Shirl Anderson was murdered at exactly 3:05 a.m. this morning. What time did you leave her apartment?"

I no longer had to guess now. Chief McNeil considered me a key witness in the case.

"About 10 minutes after midnight, sir."

At that moment, Detectives Jones and Olerhy walked into the office. "Yeah Chief - Mary said you wanted to see us?"

"I just wanted you to participate in an interrogation," He glanced at me. It was obvious to the detectives that I was now a prime witness. The questioning began:

"What's your exact address?"

"4852 South Prairie Avenue. First floor in the rear."

"Are you originally from Chicago?"

"No, I'm originally from Robbin, Illinois." (I had to make that a good one).

"How long have you been living in Chicago?"

"About five years."

"How long have you known Shirl Anderson?"

"I met her exactly two nights ago."

"And did you pay for her services?"

"Yes, I did."

"So it's fair to say that on the night of August 4 1966, you were with Shirl Anderson?"

"Yes, that is true...look, what's with these questions, huh? Surely you don't think I had anything to do with it, do yah?"

"What were you doing exactly a week ago today, Mr. James?"

"I was trying to find a job."

"Where were you living at that time?"

"I wasn't, I was drifting."

"Do you think Aaron Wilkins murdered Shirl Anderson on the night of August 4th, Mr. James?"

"Yes. I saw dried blood and bloody footprints in front of his door that morning!"

"How long did you stay at her apartment, Mr. James?"

"About five hours."

"That means you arrived there about 7:30pm?"

"That's right, we had consensual sex. I didn't rape her. Why these asinine questions?"

"What makes you think she was raped?"

"Detectives Olerhy and Jones told me so."

"How did you happen to be in the area? I mean, we already know that you just recently moved into that building."

"I told you, I'm a drifter and I was looking for an apartment in the area…and while I was walking her dog—"

"Dog? We didn't see any dog on the premises, Mr. James."

"Well, she had one. It's a small black dog." Detective Olerhy broke in. "Chief, the medical examiner did find dog hairs all through her apartment."

McNeil continued his questions:

"When you first met Miss Anderson, did you realize she was a prostitute?"

"Not until I went inside her house."

"And then?"

"Look, you want details? She asked me if I wanted to buy some ass and I did…Jeeesus!"

The chief pushed back from his desk, opened his drawer, and dumped some crumpled $10 bills on his desk.

"You ever see that money before?"

"No, I haven't."

"Now look, James, you gave her money. You were the last man to *buy some ass* from her. Now, are you trying to tell me that's not the money you paid her with?"

"That is perfectly correct, sir."

"You're gonna have a hellava time proving that it the lab boys find your fingerprints on it."

"I tell you, it's not my money."

"Okay, James, don't panic."

"I'm not panicking."

"Mr. James, do yourself a favor and take a real close look at this money and tell me if you see anything at all wrong with it."

I rose from my seat, walked over to his desk, and gazed down at the money. I knew it couldn't be the illusory money because that would dematerialize in 15 minutes. But I did notice that all the money had the same serial numbers. I quickly wondered if Shirl was involved in a counterfeit ring.

"Well, Mr. James?"

"It's counterfeit money."

"That's right, and you claim you have never seen it before."

"Look, I don't know. Maybe I did see it unknowingly. But jees-us, you expect me to check every dollar I have?"

"Mr. James, we're going to let you go. But if you so much as ride the bus in the wrong direction, if you so much as fart too loud, we're going to lock you up for using counterfeit money. You understand that?"

"Yes, you made that very clear, sir."

"You damn well better understand. Now you can leave. But expect repeated visits until this case is solved. Remember, without you, we have no case!"

I walked out of the police station and headed toward the bus stop as a cool Lake Michigan breezes lowered the heat. I smiled as I thought about how I had helped to find Shirl's killer.

After I got off the bus, I walked down the street toward Teresa's Lounge on 46th and Indiana Avenue I felt faint the heat was suffocating. I wanted to relax and cool off. Teresa's is a small lounge that caters to a black and white Blues and Jazz crowd. I had been there once and became so impressed with the exotic music that I went back every time I got a chance to hear it.

The Color of My Blood

It was a small lounge in the basement of a large tenement building. At the end of the lounge was a small platform for the performers. The bar was short and parallel to the rectangular room. The room reeked with cheap perfume, reefer, intermixed with smoke and muted voices.

As I walked into the crowded lounge, the power of the *Blues* enveloped me. A mournful organic quality streamed from the electric guitar of a huge black man, who started to sing with a deep, raspy voice. In back of him a sign read: *HOWLAN' WOOLF.*

I sat down behind the lounge. I ordered a cold beer still reeling over Shirl's death. I shuddered as the bluesman's mournful voice conjured up images of my dead son's cry for help. I listened:

"The dog began to bark. Hounds began to howl, oh dah' hounds began to howl ah' watch out yah' people 'cause dah' little red rooster on dah' prowl!"

John Sibley

USS OBAMA 2112

Date: November 6, 2112

United States Marine Galactic Force USS Obama

Destination: Solstice Galactic Prison, Proximal Centauri

Distance: 4.3 light years from Earth

My name is Captain Toussaint Barack Williams. I am 32 years old and I stand about 6 feet, 3 inches tall. My father is African American and my mother is both Irish and Cherokee, with a smidgeon of Chinese.

I was teased in grammar school because I was poor. Poverty and classism was the new racism. I was an exception because most poor children could not compete with the *desigs* -- what they use to call designer children. Their upper-class parents could afford to put genechips *invitro* to increase their intelligence.

My generation was called *mixolattoes*. We were mutts. So if you mixed R&B, Irish jig, Pocahontas, and Mao Tse Tung, and every other ethnic gene, you get Captain Toussaint Barack Williams, a career officer in the United States Galactic Force (USGF). I was selected for the General Chappie James Leadership Academy on September 6, 2080. At 23, I received my nine-year advanced officer training in Military Galactic Security Systems Leadership on the Terra IV Sac Wing of the USS PROTEUS starship. Admiral William "Wolf" Armstrong promoted me to captain last year.

All that training taught me that life on Earth is not very special, and our species is not fundamentally much different from all the others in the universe. It also taught me that a living organism based on Ammonia and hydrogen, rather than water and oxygen, could have a conscious mind like humans. That reality was critical in becoming an officer in USGF because it removed the intellectual foundation that somehow, earthlings are superior, or that earth is a special place.

The USGF is part of a joint-federation of advanced planets, with a charter protecting the rights of humans and non-humans with trade and ethical rules. This encourages and enforces fairness and transparency.

To think that on November 6, 2012 -- 100 years ago -- a distant relative of mine, Barack Obama (what a name!), was re-elected President of the United States. My father's great, great grandfather, Lieutenant William Alonzo Williams of the USAF, married Obama's oldest daughter, Malia, who was 14 years old when they met in high school in 2016. Sasha, Obama's youngest daughter (her real name was Natasha), also married, and was later chosen as Secretary of State.

When I was growing up, I spent a lot of time sitting with my great Grandma Malone. She was 200 years old when she opted to die. She won the "The Telo Life Lottery." It was a prize that gave winners yearly *telomere* therapy, which kept healthy telomeres (the protective ends of chromosomes) healthy, which are linked to ageing cells. Her lottery therapy postponed death for 130 years. But like so many other seniors that won the yearly prize, she became disillusioned with replacement hearts, livers, kidneys, and fading memory pills. Grandma Malone's prize, she realized, could not make her immortal. She ultimately became tired of getting cloned organs and titanium hip replacements. She died peacefully at the Heavenly Ashbury Senior Home on October 1, 2112 -- one second before a dramatic total eclipse plunged the sun into darkness for four minutes.

She told me that my great, great, great grandmother was named Deloris Malia Williams. Through my DNA, I know I share the same genetic bloodline as Malia Obama. Grandma Malone used to say, with ancestral pride, that the blood of America's first Black president is coursing through my veins. On my father's side, I knew very little, and I never knew my paternal grandfather.

USS Obama 2112

Home for me was the Southside of Chicago. We lived at 4852 M. L. King Avenue in a horseshoe-shaped edifice we called *Cabrini,* which had 500 apartments, an organic farm, stores, and a hologym. It was a self-contained subsidized housing for the poor. It was a mixed-used community where I played basketball and walked my bot-dog, Ming. Gangs and crime were under control because of a GPS microchip placed under your skull, which could identify you from birth. This was along with cameras embedded in painted walls, which could show any criminal hard at work.

I had four older sisters and one older brother, but they all died from the XAIDS Plague of 2080, and both my mother and father are dead and gone now. Sometimes I get very depressed about it and I still very much miss that old neighborhood. Chicago was once a beautiful seasonal city.

But a 2 degree Celsius increase in global temperature had made Chicago's summers a hellish environment. Its scorching heat wave has caused over 20,000 heat-related deaths. Lake Michigan's temperature would sometimes reach boiling point. Recent reports are encouraging, because solar wind and geothermal renewable energy caused global temperature to cool down. But the heat waves in Chicago were nothing compared to California's 8.2 on the Richter scale "Big Quake," which killed 350,000 people in 2087. It destroyed power lines, railroad tracks, and the city's total infrastructure was mangled. Over 100,000 California refugees fled and came to Chicago.

I will never forget Dr. Cornel Crestifo, PhD., who was my teacher back in 2094 for mathematics, history, and science at Crane Westside Math and Science Prep High School. Dr. Crestifo was from Nigeria. His resume was impeccable; there were even rumors that he might one day receive the Nobel Prize in Physics for challenging and debunking Einstein's Theory of Relativity. His skin was blue-black. So black that up close, you could see the blue sky reflecting on it. Everywhere he walked, people stared. He was very proud of his dark melanin skin. He even wrote a book about how melanin affects the human body; but the book didn't stop the students from nicknaming him "Dr. Poot" because they jokingly said he was black enough to poot smoke.

He was a short bald man of medium build in his late 40s. His large, bottle-thick eyeglasses and slightly crossed eyes made him appear all knowing. His large African lips, as pink as newborn mice, gave his face a cartoonish, yet scholarly quality. Only the top 1 percent of students were in his class because it was so rigorous; a class he described as seeking to teach the organic unity of math, science, and history. He would ask me questions like "Toussaint, what's the difference between killing worms and buffaloes?" I would answer, "The difference is in scale, not principle."

I remember my first day in Dr. Crestifo's physics class. I will never forget how all his handpicked students were captivated by his brilliant words.

"Students, it is important that you remember the name of Dr. Gabriel Aude Oyibo, who was a Nigerian mathematician and physicist like myself. He solved the Grand Unification Theory -- popularly known as 'the theory of everything,' or the holy grail of mathematics and physics, in 1990, by discovering the GOD Almighty's Grand Unified Theorem. Dr. Oyibo won the Nobel Prize for his GAGUT Theorem in 2016, and was the first African to win the prize.

In simple language, GAGUT states that GOD, everything including the Unified Force Field, or any fundamental force or particle interactions, is conserved with a transformation process over space and time, which cannot be disputed by ANY logical process.

We will use Dr. Oyibo's GAGUT theory in this class as a template for studying physic problems. Keep in mind all of you were handpicked for this advanced physics class, so I wish you all the best."

Without Dr. Crestifo's mentoring, I never would have graduated from the United States Marine Galactic Academy. After all these years I still wonder what my mother was thinking about, watching me proudly as I graduated first in my class. If I shut my eyes tightly, I can still see her face, tears streaming down her cheeks, when the auditorium surged with energy as we threw our hats in the air with jubilant celebration. I can still see her standing up and holding her hands as if she were praying as she smiled at me.

I miss my wife, Laura, my son, Barack, and my two daughters, Jaqueline and Brittany. I even miss my bot-dog Ming and all of my friends. I definitely miss the cobalt-blue sky of earth. In space, there is no day and night. There's no sunrise. There's no billowing clouds, fog or haze. No Lake Michigan. No fireflies. I still sometimes get motion sickness from the side effects of artificial gravity. Even when I take a leak, the stream is like a curve ball. We also have to monitor our red blood cell count, because it will drop. I do like having sex with the sex-bots in zero-g. But artificial sex is fleeting. Nothing has stopped me from sometimes getting on my knees and asking God to fill the hollowness of my heart and soul. I need something that can fill the void of my constant thoughts of my family on Earth. Sure, I can go into the Holo Theater and trick my mind and senses into walking barefooted on the sands of Congo Beach in Chicago, but that would be just an illusion.

This is my first assignment as Captain of USS OBAMA, where there are currently 500 soldiers marooned together onboard. Our mission is to stop a prison insurrection at Solstice Galactic Prison. SGP is a reconditioned military starship, a maximum 3 Galactic Security Prison used to house the most wretched, murderous, and barbaric inmates -- both human and alien -- captured in different star systems. We will board SGP four hours from now. Since some of these prisoners are more advanced than humans, I had to handpick my crew because there is no time for cowards or nervous nannies.

My crew includes my two bot–dogs, Ying and Yang; Mula, my half-alien-human navigator; Ali, a huge 500-pound metamorph B alien from the Tau Ceti star system where they are bred to be warriors; and Dr. Love, our humanoid medbot. I only wished they hadn't sculpted Dr. Love's face like the famous popstar, Michael Jackson. His face is porcelain white, almost marble-like. It looks like polished bone.

Stromwell is our chief engineer of the ship and Sergeant Henchmon is the platoon leader. He's a true soldier. He served two years on the Mission 6 colony on Saturn's tiny water-rich moon Enceladus, fighting some of the most deadly aliens we have ever encountered. My weapons' squad leader is a homeboy from Chi-town, Calvin "the Real Deal' Jenkins, who was stationed on Saturn's larger moon Titan for two years and reputed to be the best weapons soldier on any starship.

Now, as when they did in 2012, when my distant relative President Obama was fighting terrorists, we still have a need for security forces to suppress rebellions, terrorists, galactic pirates, alien slavery, and stopping the spread of Galactic Zoos.

My mother said that I was born into action because she gave birth to me on January 2180, the same day that the Russians discovered Somellow, a galactic ore that once distilled becomes a powdery addictive drug that wars are fought over. The irony is that it was found in a mining colony on Mars.

If the United States, Russia, Africa, and China had never started a space colony race for power, prestige, and controlling the world's energy grid, I wouldn't be thinking about a blue sky, birds, and Congo Beach on the Southside of Chicago. The U.S. and China both started their moon colony at the same time. First, it was the two colonies, with each having 5,000 American and Chinese moon miners to build the living quarters. Then they built the power stations on the moon so the miners could launch raw materials back to earth. In just 5 years, the Americans and the Chinese had built power satellites that could deliver 5 million kilowatts of power to Earth. After the depletion of moon resources, Mars was next, after Mars, resources were gathered from a satellite of Saturn, named Titan.

Then something truly spectacular happened. A scientist by the name of Sonuki discovered a loophole in Einstein's theory, which stated that using a negative energy bubble as fuel could warp the fabric of space and time. This enabled military starships like the USS OBAMA to reach planets 12 light-years away in half the time.

In 2095, an alien ship crashed on Earth in Norfolk, Virginia, with 100 homeless alien slaves that were being shipped to a Martian colony to mine Somellow. The minute they exhaled Earth's oxygen, quarantining them was useless. The bacteria from their lungs wiped out close to a billion humans. It was the worst epidemic in Earth's history. That epidemic caused the First Alien War, which lasted 30 years. It also caused Mountain and Plain states like Colorado, Texas, and Utah, to secede from the United States of America and form the Western Axis. I was lucky I was inoculated with the serum -- my mother said it made the old XAIDS disease seem like Chicken Pox. She said millions died before a serum was developed to cure the disease. She always told me to thank the Lord for that serum.

The First Alien War created a galactic labor shortage. Slavers from the Hound Dog Star System resorted to raiding other worlds for galactic slaves, mostly aliens from Proximal Centauri, the closest of the triple-star system to Earth. Epsilon Eridani, 61 Cygni, Epsilon Indi, and Tau Ceti, all are a mere 12 light-years from Earth. The slaves from Alpha Centauri were called "Glavs." They, along with others, were used to mine the Somellow plant on Mars.

- ◊ -

John Sibley

Rozale's Illustrated Encyclopedia of Galactic Drugs

SOMELLOW

Hellas Planitia Somellow

Martian Somellow is a pharmaceutically gifted plant. It has a history as a galactic drug that can treat and cure all types of planetary diseases. However, its side effects can mean instant death.

Description

It is a spiky-looking plant. Somellow feeds off the nutrients of the carnivorous Martian flytrap leaves: oblong, deeply divided, upper leaves are attached. Tea made from the leaves is believed to slow down aging.

History

The active principle in the root of Somellow is thujoint, an alkaloid that causes addicts to inject, sniff, smoke, and even rub Somellow on their body because thujoint has the same effect on the reception sites in the brain as THD (tetrahydrocannabinol), the active principle of marijuana and cocaine. Researchers at Galactic Pharm Company, in search of an anti-aging drug, have found that extracts of Somellow leaves could prolong the life of 90-year-old seniors up to 20 additional years.

Uses

In 2031, American chemist James Frisele, M.D., wrote an article about Somellow in the Galactic Journal. Immediately after, pharmaceutical companies' robotic probes were sent to Mars, searching for *Hellas Planitia Somellow* and its relative. It did not take the pharmaceutical companies long to discover that the Alien Food and Drug Administration, AFDA, considered Somellow an unsafe drug.

Somellow is the source of 100 medically significant alkaloids, especially thujoint. It is also the source of galactic war, colonization, and slavery by pirates from the Aldebaran, Arcturan, Pleiadian, and the Hound Dogs constellation, Canes Venatici. If it were not for the intervention of the United Worlds Confederation, subterranean Mars would be a barren wasteland today.

The Xenoi Star System has the best galactic slave market in the galaxy. The Xenoian beings are able to breathe CO_2 through gills in their necks, which made them valuable workers in the dark Martian environment. Their dark, scaly viridian skin is layered with enough fatty tissue to protect them from the Martian heat. Their ability to convert anaerobic bacteria from Martian soil as a food supply increased their value, and made them the strongest and healthiest slaves in the galaxy.

The lighter colored female Xenoians, called Xenopree, were used for mating; the Xenoiffe, mid-viridians, were used as managers, and the male Xenostiffs, the dark-viridians, were used to cut and pick the Somellow plants. Martian Somellow labor was so harsh that galactic slaves were only healthy for two Earth years, upon which they were then shipped to partake in lighter work on the iron and magnesium-rich mines on Mars' two moons, Phobos and Deimos. Mars served as a planet of transit for Glavs taken throughout the Alpha Centauri Galaxy. That was until the USS OBAMA and other GUF Galactic Union Fleets disrupted the chain of supply.

"Captain Keyes, I need you on the bridge," Mula, my half-human female alien, and the celestial navigator, whispered through my collar phone.

"Mula, I'm on my way!" I patted the head of my two guard dogs Ying and Yang. Dim light slathered the metallic canines' teeth. Their eyes, lacking any pupils, glistened crimson. In order to graduate officer training school, we had to pass a class on how bot dogs were indispensable in detecting laser gun fumes, not detectable by humans. They can also sniff out alien chameleon creatures, and galactic drugs; and you don't have to deal with dog shit. Ying and Yang's state-of-the-art positron-cog-brains were modeled like a real dog's brain; but instead of convoluted brain tissue, there was a system of holo-transmitters, switches, nano-neurons, and arti-synapses. Real dogs have about 10 million neurons in their brains. Ying and Yang have about eight billion.

As I walked into the control room, I couldn't help but marvel at her beautiful ass. She was half Xenopree, the light viridian female Glavs, used for mating. They are crossbred to eliminate the bacteria in their lungs, which wiped out close to a billion humans in 2095. But her anatomy was not structured for a human male. I often wondered if inside she struggles with being both human and alien. I wondered if something inside her wanted to emerge, like a grub coming out of a cocoon. I wondered what her *brain print* would look like. It was difficult for all the males on the ship to believe she was not human. Her sexual aura made all the men on the ship uneasy -- even me.

I glanced out at the milky blackness of space out of our command room window. Mula's owl-like eyes twinkled as she turned around and smiled at me. She was whistling some ancient song. I clicked on the music library in my *aug* collar. The name of the song was *"My Favorite Things"* by John Coltrane.

"Great song Mula," I said.

"Coltrane's music is magical, isn't it? John Coltrane was an alto jazz saxophonist way back in the '60s."

"An alto what?" I asked perplexed.

"An alto saxophone jazz musician," Mula explained. "He came up with the theory of GOD's music." She reached out and touched my left cheek with three webbed fingers and a thumb, and one human finger. Her nails were blood red and shaped like eagle talons. She was an empathy...they can touch your soul with their hands.

She whispered, "The music has calmed your emotions, don't you feel it? His music was so spiritual and universal. He was light-years ahead of his time. His music calms *all* souls in the universe."

"I prefer the P-Funk of the *Mothership Connection* by Parliament Funkadelic!"

"To each their own...you like George Clinton's P-funk mythology over John Coltrane, huh?"

"Definitely. Now, mission update, Mula?" I asked.

"Sir, we will link up and swing around SGP in a loose parabola and send a shuttle platoon, as you instructed, to squash the insurrection. We must be cautious because the leader of the rebellion, Elijah Comen, is threatening to blow up SGP if we come aboard without accepting his demands. The platoon's cargo will consist of weapons and miscellaneous equipment. The detachable space jets, orbiters, and robo-probes are activated. We will attack with your command."

"I will contact Colonel Henchmon to prepare the infantry platoon. I don't give a shit about Elijah's demands. Either they surrender or we annihilate them."

The passing of the Galactic Transportation Act in 2112, by the United States and the Galactic Confederation, made it legal to house Earthen convicts, alien pirates, kidnapped Glavs (alien slaves), and captured galactic zoo creatures (some smart, some idiots) at SGP. Thousands are corralled and shipped to SGP under the Act, along with scum and dregs from other worlds.

I knew that Elijah Comen would be a formidable foe. He was a messianic leader. Authorities on Earth said he reminded them of a galactic Lenin because, like him, he realized too well the need. the obsession to have a secret organization that monitors others. He needed to watch his internal and external enemies of his galactic drug cartel, and the Solstice Galactic Prison had become his base of operation, like the Lubyanka building in Moscow was for Lenin.

Squashing his rebellion on SGP would not be an easy task. I needed to update my information on him and his gang.

I walked into the Cyber Theater and sat down in front of the Military Archival Robotic Computer. "MARC, I need data on Elijah Comen, inmates, and the general population of SGP."

The lights dimmed in the Cyber Theater -- three-dimensional colors stung my eyes. MARC's computer-generated voice spoke as Elijah Comen's face beamed a meter in front of me.

> **Name:** Elijah Comen
>
> **Aliases:** William Butler, John Henson, Jeff Wilburn
>
> **Description:** Born in Chicago, 11-22-2090
>
> 6'3"; 210 lbs.
>
> Brown eyes, dreadlocks
>
> Dark brown complexion
>
> Knife cut on left cheek
>
> **Localities:** Deported to SGP 1-28-2109

Comen has been in prison for half of his 40 years. He is serving a 100- to 300-year sentence at Solstice Galactic Prison after being convicted in 2102 of killing an alien union steward for interfering with his Somellow cartel.

I remember when I was just 15 years old in 2065, how a radical friend of mine, Henry Mathews, took me to see the messianic leader, Elijah Comen. Back then, he was an activist for global rights. I never will forget that hot May night at Chicago's Soldier Field. I can still hear the thunderous roar, and the mantra-like chant of the stadium crowd.

> *"We want Elijah! We want Elijah!"*

I remember the crowd making a human wave while holding placards, banners, and flags written in bloody red. They were shouting,

"War notes...war notes...forever!"

Elijah wrote WAR NOTES, his 500-page manifesto and a series of lectures and philosophies, for his followers. He wrote the book while serving a five-year sentence at the "Big Max" -- a maximum-security penitentiary in Colorado -- for plotting to blow up a galactic mining freight that used alien slave labor. The book demanded an armed revolution by any means necessary; to destroy all life in the galaxy based on greed and exploitation...

"We will unite the galaxy against the evil-doers. We must cast off the yoke of capitalist growth at any cost, and liberate our galactic brethren from the blood-sucking leeches!"

His manifesto was, and still is, an underground classic. I still don't understand how such a charismatic leader could turn into a renegade, a merchant of death. Here he was peddling an addictive drug to potential followers. I snapped out of my thoughts as another face beamed in front of me.

Brian Akins, 22 -- Criminal Drug Conspiracy

Michael "Jawbreakers" Allegro, 35 -- a loyal enforcer for Elijah.

Terrell Harris, 32 -- a galactic mule for Elijah.

"Antron is a dangerous bot-felon programmed to deliver drugs via space jets to planets too hazardous for humans. Like Tau Ceti, HR7703, Delta Pavonis, and Sigma Draconis..."

"MARC, did you say Sigma Draconis?"

"Yes, Captain."

"But I thought it had a sun-like Earth?"

"Not exactly, sir; it has peach-colored cumulus clouds from a methane-produced landscape in the lower atmosphere. Draconian aliens on this oceanic world live on what we call "Crater Island." A blood-red moon orbits its sun-like double stars. Draconians crave the Somellow drug. They are truly galactic addicts. They exchange sagorium cobalt magnets for their drug needs. On a brighter note sir, the planet does have rainbows from water droplets from a double star."

"MARC...so far, we have the leader Elijah Comen, Akins, Jawbreakers, Terrell, Antron -- who and what else should we be concerned with?"

"Kellogg, an alien from HR7703, is a real threat. He gained galactic notoriety in 2092, when he hacked into the United Galactic Federation Command (UGFC). He was convicted in 2094 of computer fraud, wire fraud, and attempts to hack into a negative energy RD facility on Titan. He was on the GBI's (Galactic Bureau of Investigations) Most Wanted List."

"Anything else I need to know before I go to the chow hall?"

"A large population of captured wild alien creatures on board that Elijah might use as a fortress as a last defense. He might even use them as a blockade, and then let them loose as a shield to protect his gang. Captain, all these creatures are from star systems no farther than 12 light-years from Earth. They have different traits. Some are carnivores. Some are grazers. Some are used for labor. Some are captured and used by galactic circuses for entertainment. Others are shipped to galactic zoos. Some are instinctual killers. They are bred to kill and be killed in galactic arenas -- like in ancient Rome."

"MARC, are any of these creatures sentient? Can we communicate with any of them?"

"Captain, Watar Muddy is serving time at SGP for selling Marticoke and Somellow. However, he is well known throughout the galaxy for his music. He can communicate with the creatures with it. *That old earthman adage is still true: It soothes the wildest beast. Look at this short HOLOTUBE of Watar Muddy."*

At that moment, the holo-screen flashed on.

"The galactic blues..." Watar Muddy's slithering voice wheezed as he tuned his disacoudistar with his three-snarled bony, blue-fingered hand. "Has a rhythm. It's a rhythm that defies time and space; a rhythm that is felt by being in the Vega Star System and even the warlike Devilocs in the Denebola system."

Watar Muddy's slit nostrils started to flair. His wide primate mouth gaped, showing sharp, jagged fangs. His larger upper saucer cranium swelled as all Civiligs did when they became emotional. His dark translucent spotted skin: a mélange of moss green, pink, sepia, and cobalt blue, seemed translucent as they floated underneath. He plucked another note on the disacoudistar.

"The sound was discovered on the Voyager spacecraft on a 12-inch gold-plated copper disk containing sounds and images selected to portray the diversity of life on Planet Earth. It was recorded in a primitive analog form. The Voyager launched many light years ago.

"It is this particular song, *Dark Was the Night*, by an earthman named Blind Willie Johnson, which has revolutionized how beings across the galaxies react to sound. Little did this earthman realize the power of his music on galactic souls: the moans, the exotic melody, the agonizing cries, and the heartbreaking wails. A sound evokes meaning to life on all worlds. It is like the *whoosh* of the Doppler affect as a meteorite whizzes through a solar system.

"I often wondered what type of earthman Blind Willie Johnson was. The sound of his music evokes pain, sorrow, and joy. His life journey must have been heroic, and yet tragic."

Watar Muddy's three hearts thumped loudly. A puddle of green liquid surrounded his hoof-like feet.

"The structure of his music has aroused profound attention throughout the galaxies. His music has made us question the very moral concepts that govern our Galactic Union. We are now seeking a new rhythmic paradigm. One based on a blues sensibility; a particular idea based on the harmony, improvisation, and spirit of Blind Willie Johnson's music. A concept based largely on the sound and energy that are transmitted when I pluck this note from *Dark Was the Night.*"

Gripping the disacoudistar, he stood into a crouched position. His legs were inverted, like a kangaroo's. Tremulously, he started to sing. Particles of metallic light ignited, shimmered, and glowed as his snarled fingers struck the airwave. His fingernails sparkled like carnival lights.

"I remember a long time ago when I was serving time at Vega Galactic Prison in the Hound Dogs constellation, Caines Venatici, for selling Marticoke. I heard these black earthmen singing this strange, mournful, and hypnotic song in the prison yard as they stacked lithium crystal ore dug up from the mines. I don't know what the words meant, but the sound enraptured me. Some of them called it the gospel. Others called it the blues. It was such a gut-wrenching, mournful cry, like the piteous moans of the Xenoians picking Somellow on Mars. An octave so high it made my three hearts pound like drums. It was like listening to the screams of the Frenoi babies in the lobotomizing room, as the eight-inch hydroderm laser injects a zombie solution into their brains, so they can be butchered and sold as gourmet meat.

"I'm going to try to sing the way it sounded while playing and listening to Blind Willie Johnson's music: *'Capn', doncha do me like you do po shine.'*"

Suddenly, puddles of green fluids bubbled from his head, dripping down his translucent face. It drizzled around his slit nose and twisted around his wide mouth. *"Drove him so hard till he went stone blind."*

- ◊ -

You won't believe what happened today in the chow hall. I was standing in line along with Major Stromwell, the engineer of the ship and I was hungrily waiting for my turn to check out the menu. I was expecting the regular menu from the colony farm: poultry, rabbit, fish, vegetables, and cakes. But to my surprise, the menu was very different.

MENU

TODAY'S SPECIALS INCLUDE:

Planetoids with mushrooms and hot gravy, extracted from the juices of the martian ocra plant.

- ◊ -

Chillingoids: the delicious intestines of the pig-like (quoids), creatures from the terra viii star system.

- ◊ -

Barbequed funkroids with simmering sauce marinated with the tiny spicy brain particles of the galula amphibian.

Major Stromwell smiled reassuringly at me as he pointed at the barbequed Funkroids. His blue eyes twinkled as he said, "Barack, you'll like those Funkroids...try 'em; I'll betcha want seconds. Believe me, Captain, I'm an old vet. In time you will get used to alien food."

"Probably, but what happened to the regular menu? This food even has a nasty stench to it!"

I felt nauseated, queasy, and faint. I thought to myself, *now Barack, you have eaten some pretty weird things in your life:*

pigtails, chitterling, pig's feet, liver and so on, but to tear the flesh off the bone of a creature from another planet, and a creature that might have been a living, thinking, sentient being like me? Why, that's just asking too much!

Major Stromwell and I sat down and I watched him as he smacked his lips and inhaled the pungent odor of his large plate of barbequed Funkroids.

"Captain, somehow the pollution-control methods stopped working. The rumor is that too much nitrogen was released in the space farm, contaminating the entire food supply. Forget about that right now Captain, and enjoy," Major Stromwell said.

His blue eyes became bulbous as he frantically placed the knife and fork in his bony hands and cut a large piece of the meat from the rib-jointed bone. He then determinedly stuck it into his mouth. I watched jagged maggot-like pieces of meat writhe and wiggle out of the corners of his mouth. It reminded me of how a fellow cadet used to say Asian women looked as they chewed on large water bugs in Vietnam.

Major Stromwell's tongue slapped his lips sensuously. A beam of light crisscrossed his abnormally high forehead. He belched. He wiped the sweat from his brow with a napkin and started cutting another piece of meat.

"It's rather tasty once you get past the smell, Captain. It's certainly not as gross as eating human flesh," He smiled sarcastically. "No pun intended -- besides Captain, low-grade organisms are about as stupid as a chicken. It's not like we are eating intelligent, sentient beings. Captain, be reasonable boy, we convert the Funkroid flesh into hydrocarbons, which cuts down on energy use. And the blood is supposed to make your widget as hard as elephant tusk. No shit. Now eat, enjoy, sir."

"Where do these Funkroids come from?" I asked curiously.

"Well," the major said, looking around the chow hall to see if anyone was listening. "Since this might be our last mission -- considering the criminals at SGP, and besides, quite soon the story about the Funkroids in the Beta Orion's Star System will leak out anyway."

"Funkroids? And that is really what you are eating?"

"We are eating, sir, we! Now take a bite, it won't kill you."

I nervously picked up my knife and fork and cut a small piece, put it in my mouth, and damn it if it didn't taste like barbecued ribs.

"I told you it's not bad, Captain. Well, anyway, sure as a cat has gotta tail. Lemme tell you about what happened when we first captured the Funkroids about three years ago," Major Stromwell said as he brushed his shaggy blond hair back to one side. He then reached into his jumpsuit pocket and got a tiny green memory pill. He tossed it into his mouth, swallowed some water and belched. Then he started his tale, while I hungrily started eating the Funkroids.

"We had scanned the atmosphere of Orrila -- the planet the Funkroids exist on -- and found that it was much too wretched and hot for humans, even with protective space suits. The landscape was gaseous with methane, and barren. It was a greenish-purplish wasteland where huge fungus-like pods floated in hot sulfur riverbeds, which were shrouded in pastel blue mists. Long, green-tentacled creatures clung to the pods. You could see their beady human-like eyes and slithering filigreed-like arms. Our scanners also detected that they were low-grace hydrocarbon organisms. Our starship's chef, a black guy by the name of Sammy Lee Wilson, jumped with joy because he had told us earlier that our meat supply had rotted away because the chickens and sheep had stopped reproducing.

"Anyway, we sent down some probes to see if there were any intelligent life forms. The probe scanners pointed toward the octopus-like creatures in the riverbeds. It stated that they were low-grade (meaning stupid, as in turkey), some of the ugliest, slimiest creatures you ever laid your eyes on. We then shuttled down two robot probes to capture a couple of the creatures. It was a relatively easy job. Within an hour, we had three of the large squirming octopus-like creatures in the decontaminant facility.

"They were a noxious green color; they were warm-blooded mammals, but they had long white tongues the color of a fish's belly that constantly flicked in and out; and their eyes...they looked so damn human, and that awful stare. It was like a snake's eyes: devoid of feeling..."

I felt wretched as Major Stromwell cleared his throat and drank some water. I knew from the pre-flight briefing and the Galactic Survival Manual that, if we stumbled across planets with edible life forms or fossil hydrocarbons, we should use them, which would in effect enhance energy conversion.

Major Cromwell snarled his lips, reached into his upper jumpsuit pocket and pulled out a brown cigarette. He lit it and blew thick bluish smoke rings toward the chow hall ceiling. I felt dizzy momentarily. Was he smoking Martian gold?

"Yeah," the major continued. "I never will forget how that alien had Sammy Lee running through the ship scared to death. Many of the old-timers can tell ya that Sammy was the best darn cook on any star ship. He could cook the strangest darn creatures you can think of -- he'd cook anything. He was the most resourceful feller you'd ever want to meet."

"Why do you call them Funkroids?" I asked, because I couldn't see any relationship with the name of the creatures and their planet.

His eyes were shining with excitement. He started to dislodge a piece of the meat that was stuck in his teeth. He worked his tongue around it until he broke it loose, and then he spat a glob of mucous green meat into his napkin. I pushed my plate away, disgusted.

"We called them Funkroids because they thrive off of those fungus pods I told you about earlier," he squashed the butt of his marigold into a mound of tentacle-like bones. "Yeah, those were the ugliest darn creatures I have ever laid my eyes on. Anyway, once the robot probes had the decontaminant clearance, they transported them to the storage facilities in Sammy's kitchen. We were all nervous. We had never encountered such grotesque life forms before. Sammy was petrified with fear. And believe me, Captain, Sammy had seen his share of alien life forms -- and he wasn't the weak-kneed type, either. He didn't have any punk in him. He was raised in the mean streets of Chicago's Westside. Generals that didn't have the courage and common sense of Sammy have commanded me.

"Anyway, the whole crew became jovial knowing we had a new stock of fresh meat."

I nodded my head and looked down at my plate of bones with strange little cove-shaped mounds of flesh on top of them. I wanted to puke. I wanted to run to the lavatory and regurgitate all that vile Funkroid.

Major Stromwell didn't notice my discomfort as he rambled on about Sammy. "After the robots had put the Funkroids in the storage space, I asked Sammy which alien he wanted to cook and he walked over to the glass case and pointed at a large fleshy one. I instructed the robots to put the alien creature inside the auric beam cage. Afterwards, I pressed the button and the cage turned a light blue, which was normal..." The major crossed his legs and scratched the bridge of his nose. "Well, the auric beam was supposed to disintegrate the creature's life force or soul, but...instead, that's when all hell broke loose. After I had pressed that button and the piercing auric death ray hit that critter, it started wailing, an eerie, maddening scream that echoed through the entire ship. The thing started to howl, thump, and hiss; and it actually seemed to be growing. Now you may not believe this, but Sammy Lee's hair stood straight up on his head, and I thought my heart was going to jump outta my chest. Captain, I have never seen the likes of that creature before. Then it started to coil and swing its long tentacles against the cage like bullwhips, while its other tentacles started whipping the air with a snapping sound. The cage started cracking and the Funkroid was busting out of it!

"It whipped one of its growing tentacles at Sammy. He ducked, then it started to turn a reddish blue and green while making a snake-like hiss; then it rammed its growing body against the case as one of its tentacles lurched toward Sammy as if it knew intuitively that Sammy had selected it for death."

His words made an icy cold chill crawl down my spine. I peered down at the plate of Funkroids as Major Stromwell's words scratched my ears.

"Well, by the time I could turn around Sammy was gone. All I could see was a dark blur running out of the kitchen and down the hall. He was jumpin' and shoutin' as if he had seen the devil himself. The creature outgrew the cage, scuttled out of it, and crawled down the hall after Sammy, leaving a path of jelly green fluid behind it. Sammy locked himself in the women's lavatory and that darn creature wouldn't move away from the door.

"We finally killed it by puncturing its brain with a particle beam, and Sammy cooked the crew one of the best darn meals we had ever had. But I'll be damned if Sammy touched the meat. He would not eat. I never saw Sammy again after that voyage. To this day I wonder what happened to Sammy the cook."

I felt a touch of sorrow as I looked at Major Stromwell. He fell dead silent. It was the silence you sense when a loved one had died.

He looked at me and grinned. "You look sick. You alright?"

"Stomach's a little shaky," I said.

"Well, it ain't because you enjoyed the Funkroid, that's for sure." Major Stromwell patted his stomach and slowly rose from his seat. He winked at me assuredly and walked out of the chow hall.

I leaned back in my chair. I glanced at Major Stromwell's plate. I rubbed my eyes. I looked at his plate again. I looked at mine. I wondered if my eyes were playing tricks on me. I looked again and again and again. No shit! It moved! That glob of meat he spat on the napkin wiggled. I picked it up with my fork and turned it over. Instantly, tiny centipede-like legs started to burst out of its side. The legs started kicking spasmodically. I panicked and pushed myself from the table, rising from my seat. I peered down at the thing as it started to morph before my very eyes. I saw tiny human-like eyes. I felt wretched. What had I eaten? I quickly ran to the dispensary.

What a relief. My medical report came back. I found out that Major Stromwell had been smoking Martian gold after eating his dinner, and I got a contact high and was hallucinating. The report stated that Martian Gold is made from a potent hallucinogenic herb that grows underground on Mars. I walked back into my quarters to get some rest before preparing for the last stage of our dangerous mission at SGP.

- ◊ -

Despite my years of space training, it still feels strange, forbidding, and even -- I guess the right word would be 'weird' -- to be the captain of a starship. The vastness of space makes you feel humble. It makes me feel that there is stillroom for the small voice of God. Not a Judeo-Christian God, but a God of the universe. I guess it's the same feeling my Grandma Malone had when she talked about how gazing down into the Grand Canyon on Earth made her feel like an ant on a log. My Grandma Malone said it well: Faith is the substance of things hoped for, and the evidence of things unseen.

The enormity of our mission became clear as we looked out of our space shuttle's window at SGP, a reconditioned starship looming in the distance. It looked like a rim of a bicycle tire; the shape known as a torus. It spun to provide artificial gravity for the inmates. The descent was a rough ride, but there were no hitches. We were always nervous because we all knew that a tiny crack from a meteorite could rupture the seam of the jet and kill us.

The platoon was quiet and grim. It was so quiet I could hear the solar wind blowing around the shuttle. I patted Ying and Yang and gave them a silicon bone. The shuttle's main engine howled as we reached a speed of just 320,000 km/h.

"At 11:42 we will dock with SGP soldiers. Remember people that Elijah Comen and his gang are the most ruthless killers imaginable. I repeat: there is no room for mistakes or fear," Sergeant Henchmon cleared his throat and continued. "SGP is classified as a type 3 prison, which means -- and I want to ram this into your fuckin' brains -- that it harbors not only the Earth's most diabolical criminals, but the most dangerous alien prisoners and species. Keep in mind we use SGP to hold dangerous creatures captured for galactic circuses and zoos, which Elijah will unleash on us. We are talking about prisoners that have done every imaginable crime, galactic piracy, alien slave labor, alien poachers, galactic drug cartels, even galactic pimps -- you name it, we are about to fight them!"

I gave thumbs up as we listened to the loud clutch of our shuttle jet docking with SGP. A robo-pilot started to depressurize the cabin. Pumps whirred. We all took off our helmets as a whoosh of oxygen flooded our chamber. Oxygen had a stale animal stench to it, but we were relieved we could find breathable air.

"Check your weapons soldiers," Sergeant Henchmon ordered as he clicked off his safety on his laser rifle. "Each one of your

M25 laser rifles should be loaded with 100 rounds in the magazine; and each round, when it hits them fuckers, will be like a detonating white laser heat, which will feel like a tiny nuclear bomb of hydrogen burning up their assholes -- if they have one. After each 20 rounds, a tracer will warn you that it is time to reload. You should have five other pouches on your waist loaded the same way. In case your M25 jambs -- and they sometimes do -- all of you should switch to your KEZM409 laser pistol, which is fully loaded with a 20-round magazine of laser pulsets. Any questions?"

"Hey Sarge?" specialist 4 Calhoun asked. "Are any of those fat ass Zulushians on SGP?" Everyone laughed.

"Might be, soldier," Sergeant Henchmon said. "But you better keep your dick in your pants 'cause I am sure Elijah Comen has told them to bite it off." Henchmon was the kind of leader who always made sure his men were prepared for battle. I was just happy that since we were going against Elijah Comen, a known galactic terrorist, we didn't have to follow the Galactic and Uniworld Conventions in terms of weapons. This meant we could use our total weapon arsenal.

Elijah Comen's demands were for us to provide shuttle ships that would take his gang to BECCA 3, a planet in the Centauri Rim; that's where he could make homestead claims on a mother lode of sargorium ore. BECCA 3 had the most concentrated source of the ore ever found. It is essential mineral for fusion engines, just like fossil fuel was for combustible engines. Elijah wanted all the mineral rights to be deeded to him for 100 years. He wanted to corner the market by any means necessary.

- ◊ -

"What does it feel like to kill a human Elijah?" Isuris, his loyal Zulushian female companion asked.

"I don't know what it's like!"

"Didn't you kill General Saradis, the union steward in 2102 for interfering?"

"Enough Isuris, you don't know what you are talking about!"

Zulushian females enjoyed being controlled and directed. They were highly intelligent and linguistic. She was fluent in all earth and most alien languages. Yet once they loved you, like the black widow spider, only death was the way out. They were the only female aliens that could mate with human males.

"General Saradis was not human. He was an alien like you. An alien from one of the most wicked planets in the universe." Her face was like a human female's, except for owl eyes and a lizard nose.

"I'm sure you have heard of the Sigma Draconis B star system?" Elijah said as he glanced out the navigation room window, which was close to the docking ports and could scan surrounding space for incoming crafts like the USS OBAMA Jets.

"Yes," Isuris said as she walked over to him and grabbed him around the waist. "It's a planet like your Earth-green with chlorophyll, blue oceans, bellowing white clouds. Yet home to the most vicious Killers ever known!"

"How true Isuris," he replied as he rubbed the back of her smooth, but scaly hand. "Draconis B is a haven for galactic pirates, prostitutes, poachers, and captured slaves, and once a playground for the notorious-planet-sponsored rogue General Saradis. Popular folklore says God created him so the universe would always know what evil is. This fucker made Hitler seem nice and cuddly. He was so powerful that Dragnoid natives are still singing with joy about his death. His barbarity and brutality is now a part of the cultural DNA of the solar system."

"So he was a sociopathic killer, and you, my dear," she stuck her long forked serpent tongue around his neck, licking his lips. "Are more of a freedom fighter than a killer!"

"I once was, but I did the universe a favor by killing him with these hands." Elijah closed his eyes for a moment as her hot breath flowed over his neck. He still had nightmares about Saradis's slitted reptilian eyes, expanding like balloons, as he strangled him. He thought how he woke on sweaty sheets after reliving how the yellow-greenish blood dribbled from his eyes and his skin became the color of a pale lemon as he choked the life out of him. One more evil trophy he could make a holo-pic of, that he had rid the universe of such an unsavory being.

"That's him Isuris," he clicked on the holo-pic band on his wrist.

"He was an ugly fucker!" She frowned.

"All my life, my loyalties have wavered between the seeking of wealth and justice for the underdog. The year before the Galactic Federation elected General Saradis as the union steward, he quickly killed his way to the top. He made Dragonis B his colony. The workers' conditions under his regime worsened. When I landed there to negotiate and end the strike, I was shocked by the overwhelming stench and pestilence of the worker-camps. Contract laborers from many planets had ventured to Dragonis B to mine *sargorium*. They worked all day in knee-deep Dragonian mud. I arrived in the midst of a violent dispute between various alien factions and Saradis's managers. He sent in his troops and massacred a quarter million workers to quell the violence. Then he broke all the rules and made the workers slaves by armed force."

"And what did you do?" Isuris asked nervously.

"Me and my trusted comrades, Jawbreakers and Antron, hired a boat guide and headed straight to what the alien slaves call *Slave Island*. General Saradis's shining palace sat on the planet's west coast like a beacon. A glowing castle reflected the ethereal light from a cobalt-blue lake. After anchoring the boat, we started to march to the castle, as our boots crushed the skulls and bones of alien slaves that probably tried to escape *Slave Island*. We quickly killed his guards and I told my compatriots to wait for me as I sneaked into the castle, and then I strangled him to death with my bare hands."

"So you enjoyed killing him!"

"After the lion kills the hyena, the buzzards eat the carcass and process the protein, then excrete it, returning the nutrients back to soil!"

"You mean like the dung beetle in Africa?"

"Exactly, and Saradis's evil body will do the same on *Slave Island*! Isuris, I was a revolutionary fool in my youth. Back then, I honestly believed in M. L. King, Mao, Gandhi, and even Obama's vision. I actually believed in leaders like King, and Mandela's vision of a peaceful world. But space travel has proven that *evil* is a constant in the universe. Darwinian selection rules the universe. You see it on every planet. The weak perish and the strong survive. We now know that the Homo sapiens species is not the only parasite in the universe! And yes, I did enjoy killing him."

"So you would have liked to watch the classical games in Rome's *Flavian* Amphitheater? The violence of gladiators and slaves pitted against tigers and lions would have been a metaphor of the universe for you."

"Isuris, some life forms deserve their fate. I would never hurt a baby, or you," her serpentine tongue tickled his ear.

"We must go now," he held her hand tightly. *I would kill to keep her*, he thought. *The way she loved me was magical. No human female can compete.*

"Isuris!" I snapped as we walked down the corridor to the meeting room. "Have you succeeded in gaining the personal access codes to the Galactic Market Network?"

"It will take some time to break the codes to GMN that will open up the encryptions but it will be soon!" She said nervously.

"You must break the encryption before we arrive on BECCA 3. Reading the GMN market is critical for our goal. I adore you, but I don't want you to become a victim like the gladiators and slaves in Rome's *Flavian* Amphitheater!"

Her scaly skin darkened as she wondered if Elijah would feed her to the Snappers locked in cages in the bowels of the ship.

"There is honor in death! There is no honor in being a coward!"

His voice echoed off the walls as everyone stood up and he and Isuris walked to the center of the room. Isuris telepathically translated what he said to all aliens.

"We are all in this battle together! There are no individuals. We are one. And we are not in this alone. We have received a message from special ambassador Romenoft, the expatriated emperor of Comex B, offering a friendly greeting that his clan will help us on our mission to control and recolonize the precious ore on BECCA 3 if we help him return to power!"

"So they will help us Elijah, if we help them?!"

"Yes!" Elijah raised a remote and clicked it. The holo-screen in front of him turned on. He pointed the remote at the screen.

"This will be our new home, the mineral rich BECCA 3."

"It looks like Earth, Elijah."

"Romanolft, the ambassador of Wrendrot, is an ally of the interstellar empire called Trenolaust. They need the ore for their warships, badly. Unfortunately, they are 10,000 light-years away from us. That is why we must seize the USS OBAMA!"

Elijah paused. A pulsating silence blanketed the room. Watar Muddy, the galactic musician, spoke in his nasal voice.

"Elijah, respectfully -- I know we need to reach our goal, but that also means killing all life on USS OBAMA!"

"Yes it does. In war, some must die for the greater good!"

"Then some of us must also die!" Watar Muddy said piteously.

Elijah cleared his throat. "They are sending war shuttle jets to attack us. They will arrive soon. We will destroy all of them and the shape shifters will enter their dead bodies and take over USS OBAMA. Of course we have to clean up their dead bodies a bit!" The room roared with laughter.

"It won't be easy," Elijah said cautiously. "They are seasoned warriors that can easily kill us!"

Elijah's trusted inner-circle of comrades: Brian Atkin, Jawbreakers, Antron, and Kellogg, sat at the back of him. Justag commando soldiers stood next to Elijah: they were bred to be fearsome fighters; their bodies were dark amber and covered with armadillo body-armor that grew like scales on their skin. Their crab-like pinchers held laser weapons.

"We must succeed. Failure means death. If we control BECCA 3, we will have created a gateway into the domains of hyperspace. Once we control the sargorium ore no adversary can defeat us. Now is your chance to become conquerors! Now is your time to become immortal! Are you with me?"

"Yes Elijah!" they roared, as an evangelical fever echoed off the walls.

- ◊ -

The hull of SGP clanged and lurched as we docked with it. The cramped interior of the docking tunnel smelled like urine and feces. The huge main entrance-docking door was the only thing that stood between Elijah Comen and us.

"Captain, look!' Platoon Sergeant Henchman pointed toward the ceiling as hundreds of three-foot long tarantula-like spliders with snapping pinchers hissed at us.

"Fire!" Henchmon shouted. Bright bolts of laser pellets hit the spliders. They exploded, sounding like popcorn as their empty exo-shells crashed to the floor. A bluish slime came out of their shells.

"Soldiers," Sergeant Henchmon said. "Those spliders were mild compared to what we are about to encounter in SGP. Stay alert. Stay focused!" Two soldiers aimed arc laser welders at the door hinge and started to cut through the entrance door. A large cracking sound echoed as we crushed the spider's exo-shells under our boots.

After entering the interior of the ship, I noticed that everything had been stripped down. I glanced down a long cavernous tunnel; it curved around and then began to slope down. We reached an area that stank with both human and alien waste. All the cells and cages were open, and the walls were painted a mottled grey and pale yellow.

"Captain," Sergeant Henchmon's voice echoed from my aug collar. "I have sent assault teams through the entire ship. Once each squad is anchored in their position, we should attack!"

"I will let you know when we are positioned for the attack. Just keep giving me a GPS location for all the squads from the map we have of SGP."

"Will do captain!"

My squad walked past the open cells and cages. It was obvious to me that Elijah had let loose the most vicious caged aliens. As we kept walking, I noticed a trap door in the middle of the floor. I opened it and pointed to it for Ying and Yang to go down there so I could survey with my aug visors. I adjusted my visors for high resolution as they climbed down the stairs. Waiting for them 8 meters away was a creature that loved the taste of human flesh. The dogs wheeled and waited for my command to attack. I could see the monstrous shadow of the creature on the wall as it hid behind a large cabinet. Slowly, its head emerged from the top of the cabinet; its crab-like eyes shone like silvery metal. Its head looked like a cross between an ant and a crab. I whispered for the dogs to ferret it out from behind the cabinet. The dogs attacked from both sides, like hyenas snipping and biting at the creature's lower body. The startled creature growled and turned left and right as the dogs attacked relentlessly. I checked the image of the creature in my aug-alien species data bank:

Name: *Wobbly*

Location: *double-star system of Epsilon Aurigae*

Bipedal and carnivorous/500 pounds/warm blooded

Low-level sentient

The Wobbly snapped its razor-sharp fangs at the dogs as it moved backward toward some support beams. Suddenly, it grabbed Ying by the tail and whirled it into Yang, smashing both of them into a wall. The dogs leaped on the Wobbly's neck and spine -- I could hear the *crack* of its bones as a half-ton of pressure crushed the beast. It swung around, trying to buck the dogs off its bloody back. Then suddenly, it shuddered and fell, slamming into a wall. The dead Wobbly's glassine eyes caught my attention as I watched the bot dogs sniff its body to make sure it was dead. I patted the dogs and gave them a silicon biscuit as they climbed out of the trap door.

In just an hour of entering SGP, I thought we would have to maneuver, attack, retreat, bait, and ambush. Elijah Comen wanted us to taste the sting of his arsenal of killers.

I knew his tactic was to draw us into his hellhole and search for flaws in our character, which would allow them to defeat us.

My fingers nestled on the icy cold trigger of my *KEZM409* laser pistol, as I ordered my squad of eight men to move out.

"Captain," Platoon Sergeant Henchmon said while wiping sweat off his brow, and looking at the dead bodies of his squad lying on the bloody floor. The smell of blood and defecation was overwhelming. He looked at the back of the head of one soldier that had been bitten off by a Snapper. Human brain is a Snapper's delicacy.

"Sir, the search squad has found a huge underground tunnel loaded with open cages and cells. I bet this tunnel has honeycombs inside, in fact Captain; you are probably standing on one of them right now! We are going to need more men and the medbot ASAP!"

"Henchmon, pull your men back! I will get Dr. Love and the medbot squad down there!"

"Captain you better send the weapon squad. Looks like Elijah housed the zoo creatures down here. Snappers and Wobblies have caused most of the deaths in my squad. These creatures are wild, vicious, and like to eat human brains!"

I watched the dismembered soldiers' bodies as I listened on the aug. Some of the soldiers I knew on a first name basis: *1st Battalion, 7th Calvary: Lee Crawford, Calvin Jenkins; Alpha Company: Eliot O Brien, Travis Stevens, John Davis; Bravo Company: Carl Demond, Willie Jones, Gloria Woods, Pedro Sandrigos, and Richard O' Rourke.*

I prayed we would find their dog tags because the Snappers had bitten off most of their limbs. Suddenly, the floor underneath us started to shake. A staccato blast of laser fire reverberated from beneath the floor. My collar aug *buzzed* again. A fearful Sergeant Henchmon yelled.

"Search squad 6 sw bravo -- do you read me Captain?"

"Henchmon, reinforcement should be down there," I looked at my watch. "Right about now!"

"Fuckin' Snappers and Wobblies are killing us. We need help! We need a medbot!"

"Roger search squad 6 sw bravo...medbot and weapon squad and help should..."

"Jesus, Captain. Help just arrived! Thank God!"

"How is your ammo and head count?"

"Captain out of 200 of us there is only 50 left, plus 20 wounded. These creatures are like roaches!"

"Sergeant Johnson, do you read me? How does it look down there with your weapon squad?"

Rat tatta tat tat. He was on his knees firing his M25 laser rifle when he spoke. "We are forming a perimeter around the tunnel. We need more artillery support and medbots. These fuckin' creatures are attacking us from everywhere. It's a goddamn bloodbath down here. Blood's sticking to our boots. Elijah has unleashed these monsters on us! Those fuckin' Wobblies have to be shot in the brains, otherwise they grow new limbs and keep attacking!"

"Can you hold them back until the artillery unit gets there?"

"Holy fuck, Captain, they are finally retreating from our laser blasts! I told Willie and Charles' squads to move out -- Willie went on the right flank and Charles was on the left blasting the fuckers. Jodie spotted a column of Snappers coming from an unlocked room. We pumped and blasted laser pellets and pulsetts into the squealing Snappers after they retreated. I had Specialist 4 Thomas picking up dog tags."

"Sarg, you know what these Snapper tails will sell for at the galactic market?" Specialist Thomas said as he held up six bloody tails in the light. "Each tail has a special pattern of scales, just like the gators on earth! That's why they are so valuable!"

"Captain, the bodies are nothing but mush," Sergeant Johnson said. "Nothing but hands, arms, legs, and skin on the bloody floor. It's like a galactic poaching outpost! Excuse me!"

I watched Sergeant Johnson vomit and wipe his mouth on his sleeve.

"Jesus Christ, I just stepped on a soldier's brain and it oozed into my boot. I can't take this shit anymore!"

"Seal up the shithole tunnel doors with macro-laser blasts and you guys get the fuck out of there! Use your aug GPS to rendezvous with me!"

"Will do, sir!"

As I listened to the blast of laser and pulse guns, the deathly squeal of Snapper and Wobblies sounded like dying wild boars. The faint yell of a soldier's piteous voice echoed through my aug before I clicked it off.

"That must be its mother we killed Sarg!"

"We had to kill the motherfucker before it kills one of us!"

"But Sarg, it's just a baby!"

"Soldier, fuck the sentimental shit, it's a baby Wobbly. It will grow up to eat humans! Now shoot the bitch or face court martial soldier!"

My squad kept walking down the cavernous corridor cautiously, with M25 laser rifles on automatic and ready to fire. We approached a large door. Specialist Parker laser melted the hinges. We used the butt of our rifles to knock the door down and we looked down another long tunnel. The temperature was humid and hot. We passed some empty animal cages. The lights dimmed. I told my squad to stay close to the wall with weapons drawn and ready. Suddenly, I heard a familiar human voice as the tunnel turned black.

"Toussaint, turn back son. Your mom wants you to live!"

I wiped my eyes with disbelief. As my mother slowly walked toward me, I could see she was too solid for a holo-pic. I even smelled her perfume. It was my mom in the flesh and blood. I put my finger on my M25 rifle just in case. She slowly walked toward me. It was as if she was floating. Her arms opened as if she wanted to hug me. Sergeant Henchmon's squad had just caught up with us from the rear when he yelled.

"I see my mom!"

"We all see our moms!" a soldier hollered.

"It's an illusion! Those are meta-changers. They can shape-change into your love ones. Lock and load!"

The hooves of the meta-changers clapped on the floor as each mother transformed into a huge hyena-raptor-headed beast. They attacked, howling and baring long fangs.

My mother leapt on me as it morphed into its real body. Its heavy quadruped body slammed into my ribs, knocking me down. I was dizzy and dazed. I used every ounce of my strength to strangle it as its canine fangs dripped slime onto my face. Its eyes looked like a bunch of angry red grapes staring at me. My bot dogs attacked it from the rear, giving me time to pull out my laser knife. I jammed it deep into its gut, reached for my laser pistol and unloaded. *Bam ba bamm bam*! I shuddered as the mega-changer fell off me, dead.

"Fire!" Sergeant Henchmon ordered, the *rat tat tat* of the laser blast burned large holes into the creatures. Bluish blood, fur, and tissue exploded in the air.

"Captain," said the squadron leader, Jodie. "Do you read me?"

"Yes, Jodie, go on."

"We just broke into Elijah's operation room. He gave up without a struggle. Ali just torqued the head of the last Justin warrior bodyguard. His 500 pound Metamorph body twisted it 380 degrees. It snapped like a piece of fiberglass. They were all warrior bots!"

"Great...blindfold Elijah and his survivors, and march him to the shuttle jet!"

I felt nothing but hate for him, as I thought about the cries, voices, and faces of the soldiers his renegades had killed. I made a vow, as Captain of USS OBAMA, that once we got back to the ship, we would have a roll call in honor of the 100 soldiers who gave their lives to capture Elijah Comen and his gang on SGP.

DARWIN'S GHETTO

*Dedicated to Dr. Emiel Hamberlin,
a retired biology teacher at
DuSable High School in Chicago*

CHAPTER ONE

My name is Emiel Hambolin. I'm a high school biology teacher and I used to teach at DuSable High School on the South side of Chicago, Illinois; a public school located right across the street from the largest public housing complex in the world. Out of my classroom window, I can gaze at miles and miles of the Robert Taylor Homes (a Housing Project for low-income people); it looks hard and cold, like a concrete fortress.

I recently won the 1990 Teacher of the Year Award for my innovative work in teaching biology; in fact, I was attracting quite a bit of media controversy in regards to my teaching approach. A number of newspapers had started to publish in-depth coverage of my approach to teaching impoverished Black students biology. I think what fascinated so many people was the fact that I taught my students biology with live animals. It would be nothing in my class to see a tame boa constrictor slithering on the floor, or white mice being fed to lizards, or skunks, rabbits, a red-tailed hawk, or piranhas in my sort of tame jungle.

I tried to make my class interesting enough so that students wouldn't get bored. Besides, who wants to sleep when a live boa constrictor is slowly brushing against your socks? I used to tell the parents of my students that I try to not only teach the students biology, but I also try to teach them about life. I try to instill in them great work habits.

In other words, I try to develop the child as a whole. I always used to tell those Black students *you are somebody because you exist.* When I was fired from my job I had been teaching for 12 years - I think I was one of the first Black teachers in Chicago to initiate such radical teaching techniques.

I've been unemployed for three years now. I can't find work. My teaching credential has been suspended. I will never forget how a student by the name of Roscoe Chapworth changed my life, and damn near changed our concepts of contemporary biology. Yeah...I'll never forget that cold September day. It was the first day of school that I met the wicked genius of Roscoe Chapworth...

"Roscoe Chapworth? I repeat...is there a Roscoe Chapworth in this class?" I watched the students as they all slowly turned and started to giggle, staring at a strikingly handsome young man with a large, very curly and unkempt Afro. His face was smooth and unmarred by a hard existence. It was sort of a golden complexion that seemed as though it actually glowed. He was sitting at the last table in the rear of the classroom, busily writing something. I cleared my throat and almost screamed out his name.

"Roscoe Chapworth...is that you in the back? I would appreciate if you would be kind enough to acknowledge your name!"

The students started to laugh. I watched him as he slowly stopped writing and looked at me as though I had interfered with his private thoughts.

"You are Roscoe Chapworth, correct?"

"Yeah...technically I'm Roscoe Chapworth the Third, but I will respond to just Roscoe Chapworth."

I knew instantly that I was going to have trouble with Roscoe; after one teaches for any given period, you develop an almost uncanny feeling for highly intelligent students. I knew instinctively that Roscoe was one of those.

"Students...all of you will, at the end of this semester, walk out of this classroom with some degree of knowledge of biology. We are going to start with how biology originated, and then we will progress to Darwin's theory. Does anyone know who Darwin is?"

I scanned the class and saw a number of hands. I asked a girl who was directly in front of me.

"Okay, what's your name?"

"Marcia Wilson."

"Okay Miss Wilson, tell the class what Darwin represents."

She spoke nervously. "Well...was ah...he about evolution?"

"What do you mean 'about evolution'? You can do better than that. Okay, who knows something about Darwin's Theory?"

I glanced to the back of the room and noticed that Chapworth had gone back to his private thoughts, so I posed the question to him, hoping to make him more attentive.

"Ah...Chapworth...Can you answer the question?"

"What question?"

"If you'd listened to the question, you'd know! Now, if you can't answer the question, get up and leave...I asked you if you knew anything about Darwin's Theory."

The room had become as quiet as a roach crawling over a pillow; the only sound you could hear were the squirrels rustling in their cages.

"The year 1859 is considered the beginning of the modern era of biology because it was that year that Charles Darwin, the great British naturalist, published the Origin of the Species, in which he proposed his theory of evolution by natural selection. The theory consists of two parts: the concept of evolutionary change and the concept of natural selection. First, Darwin rejected the notion that living creatures…"

In all of my 10 years on this planet as a teacher, I never ran across such a clear, sharp, and analytical young mind. It was uncanny…it seemed as though he was gifted with total recall. I glanced around the room and noticed that the students didn't seemed as surprised as I did…I started to listen again as I slowly sat down in my chair.

"Secondly…" Chapworth continued. "Darwin said that it is natural selection that determines the course of the change, and that this guiding factor can be understood in completely mechanistic terms - terms which I personally don't believe - without conscious purpose or design. That's absurd. Also, he didn't factor in this variable: interplanetary biogenics…"

"Would you simplify the definition for the class, Chapworth?"

"I mean the transfer of different life forms by passing comets and meteor impacts. For example, the Venus flytrap *Dionaea muscipula*," he pointed at the small plant in the horticulture garden. "Did it evolve on earth or descend from outer space? We still don't understand how it evolved into a carnivorous plant. It's the only plant with an active trap to capture flies. It grows in only one place on earth - a one-mile radius around Wilmington, Carolina. Surrounded by craters, the flytrap thrives on heat and fire. Darwin's Theory can't explain this alien life form…"

A few of the students rose out of their chairs and started to clap their hands with approval, but the majority had scowls on their faces. Accolades crackled through the air.

"That's my guy…Mr. Brain!"

"That ah boy, Chappy!"

I knew intuitively that *Chappy* was certainly precocious, gifted. He was possibly a genius.

"He's an Oreo. He thinks he's White. He thinks he's all 'that' cause he knows about dead White scientists. Most sissies are smart anyway. Right, punk?"

"Bitch…I'm not a sissy. It's not my fault your parents gave you retarded DNA!"

"You calling me dumb?"

"No, I said your DNA was retarded."

The chairs screeched as Chapworth and Shalur Jofur stood up and approached each other. I quickly stood between them.

"Both of you get back to your seats immediately, and you will be suspended. That hostile energy should be channeled into your books. And you had better remember, Shalur, that being gangster is a choice, not a destiny. There will be no glorifying ignorance, despair, or stagnation in my classroom. You students must strive for excellence and keep in mind that the GPA and SAT scores for Black students are the lowest for any racial group. We now realize that low scores are not because of poverty. It's because of students like Shalur here who thinks being smart makes a boy a sissy. It's a purely anti-intellectual reaction. Well, I'm not going to tolerate that attitude in this classroom. Do you understand that? Raise your hands if you understand me!"

Only Shalur's friends didn't raise their hands.

"I want you to read chapter one because we are going to have an oral test on Wednesday. Any questions? Class dismissed. Shalur and Chapworth come here!"

Shalur walked with a thuggish swagger toward me.

"Young man," I said, adjusting my glasses. "Any more ghetto outbursts…any more making a mockery of the pursuit of knowledge…and you will be suspended indefinitely. Are we on the same page?"

His dreadlocks swung like a carousel as he nodded his head. His coal-black skin reflected in the sky blue window. A pigeon fluttered its wings in a nearby cage. A 9-foot yellow and lime green python slithered over his shoes. A raccoon hissed in its cage, showing glistening fangs; a red-tailed monkey banged frantically on steel bars.

Shalur stormed out of the classroom.

CHAPTER TWO

I watched as Chapworth walk toward my desk. I noticed that a kind of dream-like quality seemed to embellish his face, and his eyes…I had never seen a young man with such strange eyes -- they looked sinister, yet magnetic. I began to talk to him in a joking manner, to release tension between us.

"Chapworth…I must say that you are special young man."

"Thanks, but I don't think so, and you can call me Chappy."

"You don't think you are special?"

"We are all special, Dr. Hambolin, because nobody else on planet Earth has our DNA!"

"Let me clarify that, Chappy. When I say special, I meant both intellectually and physically. You showed you have courage toward Shalur's threats. Threats he can back up as one of the leaders of the Black Disciple Gang."

Chappy pointed toward the window at one of the tall high-rise buildings. "The answer is right outside your window. I live on the 15th floor of the Robert Taylor building with my mother, my younger brother Phillip, and my young sister Theresa, who has sickle-cell anemia."

"That's a disease that is definitely DNA based, Chappy."

"I think sickle-cell anemia is more of a molecular disease caused by an abnormality in the molecular structure of the red blood cells, preventing the free flow of oxygen. I want to find the cause of the abnormality in my research."

"I bet your father is proud of you, isn't he?"

"My father was a hardworking man. He was a spot welder, a supervisor. He was an innocent victim. He was killed. Mowed down like a dog because his pride was misread as arrogance. He just asked some gangbangers to move so we could get by. He gripped my hand when he died. The smell of his blood still clings to me…"

"Chappy, your sister has sickle-cell anemia and your father was murdered by a gangbanger? I salute you for being so strong and focused."

"Dr. Hambolin, my father's death is a symbol of the horror that plagues poor youth like me. My theory is that the very DNA of Black people have been altered over generations because of negative societal variables that have created an M-generation…a mutant generation. A science called epigenetics verifies this. I believe biological science is my ticket out of the ghetto. I also believe that DNA research could also help Black people rid their communities of mutants by pre-natal testing. It's the type of mutants that killed my father!"

"Okay, Chappy…and what were you studying in your notebook during class?" Chappy started to stutter as he flipped to a page in his notebook and pointed with his finger at an algebraic math equation. *The Hardy Weinberg Law:*

$$P + q + 1$$
$$P2 + 2pq + q2 = 1$$

"Dr. Hambolin, this law predicts how gene frequencies will be transmitted from generation to generation. This equation…."

"And how does this help you?" I asked, almost hesitantly, as if fearful of revealing my own terror of abstract math and being lured into discussion with Chappy, which would unmask my weakness in higher math.

"No, this equation only applies to populations that are free from mutation, migration, etcetera...."

"Very impressive Chappy, I'm seriously thinking about selecting you to be my assistant this semester."

He smiled. I knew then that he would be more at ease because of my interest in him.

"Thanks Dr. Hambolin...that would make my father happy. My family lives like hostages right across the street in those Robert Taylor projects. My father was an innocent victim, Dr. Hambolin, and a symbol of the horror that plagues our communities."

"You mean gangbangers?"

"You can call them thugs, gangsters, or hoodlums. I prefer mutants. I believe their behavior is caused by pre-natal genetic mutation and epigenetics. Dr. Hambolin, as a biologist, you are aware of quite a few examples of how the activity of genes can be affected in the long-term by environmental factors."

"Yes and no, because your theory is in a *gray* area that could be perceived as demagogic. Millions have been slaughtered under the notion that they were inferior or less than human. What you are saying is that nothing can erase or change their behavior because it is genetically based. In 1939, Hitler would have agreed with you."

"Dr. Hambolin, I'm not talking about race. I'm talking about mutated DNA. And the only answer as Lenin told his followers, and I quote: 'Cleanse the lands of Russia of all sorts of human insects, of crook-fleas, and bed bugs!'"

"He also suggested, that 'one out of every 10 idlers be shot on the spot.' Is that your final solution, Chappy? Death?"

"The welfare of the whole is always more important than the individual, Dr. Hambolin!"

As I listened to him, I detected that he was sincere; I also grasped that he was like so many other poor, gifted minority children that I had taught, both Black and White. They had a tendency to feel rejected, and their intellect alone separated them from their peers. Add that to a very anti-intellectual culture and you have chaos. I questioned him.

"Tell me, Chappy, have you always had this interest in biology or is this just sort of a passing interest?" I watched his face as it became very intense. It was as though I had said something that really upset him.

"No, all my life I've been fascinated by the natural world...no kidding! I can remember when I was speculating at just 6 years old about the physical structure of roaches. Did you know that roaches are asexual and that they reproduce by parthenogenesis?"

I tried to dismiss his burst of intellect as simply the product of a lot of reading, but something told me that was wrong.

"Chappy how old are you?"

"In relation to Earth time or intergalactic time?"

I laughed inwardly, because when I was teaching a class at the University of Chicago, one of the parents had told me that every time she called her son at school to see how he was doing he would reply, "In relation to what?" I cleared my throat, trying to conceal my interest in his uncanny brain.

"For right now let's stay with Earth time, alright?"

He laughed. "Well, most people don't believe me, but I'm 12."

"What? You mean you're 12 years old?"

"Yeah, I'll be 13 next September."

It was hard to believe…I mean he looked like he was a good 15 years old at least; he had the physical stature of a young man.

He spoke nervously. "Well, I've got to go. I'm trying out for quarterback with the school team so…ah…I'll be seeing you tomorrow. Be cool."

As he walked out of the door, I quickly picked up my phone and called the school principal.

CHAPTER THREE

"Jack...this is Hambolin. Do you know anything about a student by the name of --"

"Roscoe Chapworth?"

"Yeah, how did you know?"

"Hambolin, you're not the only teacher fascinated with this 12-year-old whiz kid whom I think is a genius."

"Well, that he is..."

"Emiel, we have had White professors from prestigious schools like the University of Chicago approaching us about Chappy. It's unbelievable! At 9 years old he could speak Swahili, German, and can count to 100 in Chinese! He has skipped four grades. He could have enrolled at the prestigious Illinois Mathematics and Science Academy in Aurora this fall. At age 11, he would be one of the youngest students to study there."

"For God sake why didn't he go?"

"They live in the Robert Taylor homes. They are dirt poor. Gangsters murdered the father when he was just a baby. His Haitian mother is fearful of her only son living alone in the White northwest suburbs without adequate financial support."

"Why DuSable? Why not the University of Chicago Lab School then?"

"Doctor, let's not forget that Chappy is a product of this neighborhood and has strong moral support. He wants to prove to the world and to the millions of people nationwide that genius is mysterious and can manifest itself anywhere. With a teacher like you, Dr. Hambolin, I'm confident that Chappy will get the right nurturing and scholarship. I think the plants and animals in your biology lab will help Chappy's genius grow, both academically and spiritually."

"Thanks, he does have a thirst for knowledge, and I want to be more than just a teacher with all my students."

"Emiel, he was in Jet Magazine at the age of 3 years old…and guess what for? Reading the Bible and it's hard for even me to get anything out of it…"

"Well, why didn't somebody inform me about this kid? I mean, at least I would have known."

"Well Emiel…it's just one of those things, that's all. But I have his records here in the office. If you'd like, I could read some of his accomplishments to you."

"Yeah…please do."

As Jack went to get the records, I sat nearly petrified with shock and I momentarily felt insecure with the thoughts of teaching Chappy. Jack came back with the records and my thoughts shattered.

"Emiel?"

"Yeah, go on Jack."

"Okay…every time I read this I feel a bit of racial pride…it's unbelievable!"

"Well, what the hell is it?"

"Now listen very closely," Jack said. I heard him open up one of Chappy's notebooks. "I'm going to read an excerpt from his notebook, which proves the boy is a bona fide genius."

"I'm waiting, Jack," I said eagerly.

"Does U-238 mean anything to you Emiel?"

"If my memory serves me correctly, natural uranium consist of two isotopes; uranium 238 is one of them. In addition, when the isotope is obtained in huge quantities you can create a huge atomic explosion. Why do you ask?"

"Listen closely to this," the principal said. "And keep in mind that Chappy was just ten when he wrote this in his notebook: *My theory to extract from natural uranium the fissionable isotope U-238, the explosive material needed for a bomb, has not been correct. Is that why the German scientists chose plutonium since its more easily extractable from a uranium reactor?*"

"You mean Chappy is toying with the notion of creating an atomic bomb?"

"He is only interested in the theory behind it, Emiel," Jack said with astonishment as he flipped through the notebook pages.

"I think Chappy is a potential genius. So far, all his ideas are based in past notions," I suggested. "Which is a moot point because he is still a child."

"Look, why is it so hard for reasonable, educated Black folks to stop viewing themselves in totally European standards? Now look, Emiel, if you don't believe Chappy is a genius, come down to my office where you can look at it in black and white. Better yet, Emiel, let me read a few of this 11 year old's accomplishments. National ranking as a teen chess player - he taught himself to play; reading at the age of two, and doing algebra at 4 and 5 years old; a perfect score on a national Latin exam; ranking 13th in the nation - are you listening Emiel? I said 13th in the nation on a physics test as a high school freshmen, even though he has never taken a physics class! And he was the first stringer on his grammar school basketball team.

Still unconvinced?"

"I'm convinced Jack, I'm a Chappy believer now!"

"It's sickening sometimes to hear the educators of our children harping on about how Black and genius are somehow oxymoronic…or they just aren't as smart as White and Asian children. Now that we have an authentic Black child genius in our midst, it's still hard for you to accept it. Look, why is it that Black folks can't produce someone more intelligent than Einstein? Damn it man, God isn't prejudiced when he gives out brains…he doesn't give a damn what color you are. You should know that genius comes in all sizes, shapes, and colors. Wake up, man!"

"Alright, Jack, I…I didn't mean it the way it sounded. I mean, it's just that Einstein was a grown man when he really started grappling with his theories…but we're dealing with a 12-year-old kid who's actually challenging Darwin's Theories. I mean it's…it's…"

"It's what, Emiel? I know what you're going to say. That is unbelievable, right? Well it's believable alright, and you had damn well better realize that this semester in your biology class. I have a meeting to go to. I'll see you tomorrow." Jack slammed down the phone.

I knew I should have been more cautious in what I had said to Jack; I just forgot that Jack was a staunch advocate of racial pride, and he should be. But I just hated it when Jack became so stormed up over speculation that he'd lose his logic, and sometimes his restraint.

CHAPTER FOUR

"Say pussy, what's up man?"

Chappy turned toward the elevator hallway door as Shalur and four of his lackeys stood motionless around him with their red baseball caps cocked to one side. Darkness blanketed the hallway; the stench of urine and reefer wafted through the air.

Chappy glanced at Shalur as he stood in the opening of the door. The contour of his body was like a painting as his silhouette pasted against the green grass and blue sky outside.

"I hear your pit-bull bitch is ready to have some pups?"

"Yeah...in a couple of weeks...bitch!"

"Bitch?"

"Yeah, you called me a pussy and I'm calling you a bitch! You like actin' tough, but that's all it is...an act! In your heart, you know you are a soft bitch. You act like a pit-bull, but you're really a lapdog. I bet you squat down when you pee...don't cha?"

"Damn, Shalur, you gonna let this wimp call you out like that?"

The elevator door screeched open. Chappy slowly walked inside. Shalur and his henchmen followed him. The door shut. A dim yellow light glowed from a broken cover, casting skull-like shadows on their faces. Gang graffiti plastered the walls. The stench of human waste was suffocating. He felt like a trapped animal. Violence crackled in the air.

"Bitch, huh!" Shalur snarled as he unzipped his fly. "We gonna see who's the bitch is now!"

The screech and clang of the elevator cables sealed his fate. He shuddered, and feeling that if he was going to die, it would be as a man and not some whimpering punk. He was not afraid. His father died with dignity. As MLK once said, "It's not the quantity, but the quality of life that matters." Besides, fear never stopped an execution.

"Hold him down!" Shalur barked. His henchman, Cochise, quickly put Chappy in a bear hug. Chappy quickly dropped and stepped out with his left foot, hitting the thug with his left elbow as his leg came up through Cochise's legs, kicking him in the groin.

Shalur grabbed Chappy's leg as he swung it up for a roundhouse. He fell to the floor as Shalur kicked him. Cochise punched him in the eye. The elevator door screeched open.

"If I don't get one of those pups, we gonna kick your ass every time we see you!" The door closed.

When Chappy walked into his apartment, the smells of candied yams, jerk chicken, collard greens, and cornbread wafted through the air. He covered his bruised, bulbous eye with his hand. His 5-year-old brother Philip and 3-year-old sister Theresa were watching television. His mother waved at him, not looking at him directly.

"Chappy, dinner will be ready in an hour. Time enough for you to straighten up that smelly room that you keep locked up!"

"Ma, you know I only keep it locked because of my science experiments in Dr. Hambolin's class. I've got some good news; Dr. Hambolin wants me to be his assistant."

"Great Chappy, but just clean up your room. The stench is polluting the apartment."

Chappy rubbed Philip's head and pinched Theresa on the cheek as he walked toward his room. As he put the key in the door, he could hear the rustling of the pit-bull pups in their cages. He had to hurry and find another place to keep them because their size was doubling weekly. But first, he must test the electrodes he had implanted in their brains so they could be steered like robotic killers.

Moonlight floated in from a nearby window over his bed as he looked around his small bedroom. The two pups banged loudly on the metal cage as they recognized him. He would have to move them tonight. Maybe one of the empty freight cars across the tracks would do.

Chappy picked up a small wireless transmitter and pointed it at the pups. Their pupils suddenly dilated as their cortical cells were stimulated. Their ears twitched. Their muscles seemed to jerk spasmodically. He pressed another button, governing aggression. The pups snarled, showing their tiny canines gleaming from the moonlight. They started banging and biting on the cage bars so viciously that their gums stated to bleed. Chappy quickly clicked off the aggressive mode sequence and the pups instantly became normal. He opened the wire cage and picked one up; it started licking his hand.

"Chappy, dinner is ready and you gonna' have to get them dogs outta' this house!"

"Alright, Ma, I'll be right out."

Eureka! The electrodes worked along with the human brain genes they now possessed. He glanced at the book on his bed and smiled. The book's title, *Toward a Psychocivilized Society* by Jose Delgado.

CHAPTER FIVE

Detective Milton Olerhy and Joe "Tank" Morgan walked down the yellow-taped, crisscrossed crime scene with disbelief. Decapitated bodies of five gangbangers were strewn across the alley. Shiny, fleshless skulls glowed as if radioactive phosphorus tracers had been injected into them. A river of blood weaved snake-like over the decomposed carnage of baseball caps and guns. A bright orange rising sun illuminated hundreds of small plastic containers of meth, marijuana, crack, and cocaine.

"I haven't seen anything like this since Nam. This is a fuckin' war zone," Tank bristled.

"Yeah," Olerhy said as he gazed at the nearby coroner's vans and patrol cars. "This is something like out of a horror movie. In my 20 years as a Chicago cop, I've never seen anything so un-human."

There was no need of a formal introduction for Detective Milton Olerhy and his partner, Detective Joe Morgan. There wasn't a criminal on the Southside who hadn't heard of their legendary ruthless salt and pepper escapades. Detective Olerhy looked more like an Irish priest; tall, average build, blue eyes, and a personable type. Detective "Tank" Morgan, on the other hand, was a 280-pound muscular ex-defensive end for the Chicago Bears, whose NFL career was cut short because of a torn ACL. He got the "Tank" moniker because he would break arms, legs, and mangle hardcore thugs in the name of justice.

"This is some sick shit!" Detective Jack Roberts, head of CSI moaned as he walked over and picked up a glowing skull. "I got eight crime techs working on this scene. The coroner's tech just left. Look at this skull. It's like the head was bitten off by a huge dog; and look at these huge canine marks," he stabbed with his fingers as

Olerhy and Tank squinted at the canine punctures.

"I already sent a skull to Dr. Lathop at the University of Chicago's Internal Radiation Department."

"Why are the skulls glowing like that?" Tank asked.

"I'm no expert Tank, but it has something to do with the radioactive material in the beast that killed them!"

A short, stocky Latino cop walked toward them with a sheet of paper flapping in his hand. "Detective Roberts, this is the report from Dr. Lathrop at the University of Chicago."

"Thanks!" He scanned the report and smiled. He nodded his head as if it confirmed his theories.

"What did she find out?" Olerhy asked impatiently.

"A huge mutant dog ripped off their heads!"

"C'mon, Jake…a fuckin' mutant dog?" Tank said incredulously.

"Um' not shittin' you, Dr. Lathrup also says that the glow is from *technetium*, a radioactive element discovered in 1930. Her theory is that whoever created these mutant mutts experimented with the isotope technetium by injecting it into the killer dogs' bloodstream and using it to possibly monitor their growth rate."

"Jake, this area is not known for producing Nobel Prize winners. Who in this impoverished neighborhood would want to monitor the growth rate of a mutant dog?" Olerhy said with puzzlement.

"I don't know…all I can tell you is that the radio tracer is normally used to help diagnose and record the size and growth of cancerous tumors. In this weird case, whoever created these beasts was very interested in their size and growth!"

"So you telling us mutant mutts killed them?"

"Tank, *killed* is too mild a word. Butchered or slaughtered would be more appropriate. All I can tell you right now is this isn't some drug-turf-crazed fight that went amok. This massacre was done by huge mutant attack dogs!"

"They were huge alright," Olerhy said as he pointed at the large bite wounds and bloody paw prints. "These dogs were more like lions or tigers in size."

"We're going to get more help from Dr. Lathrop on this one. See you guys later!"

"Yeah, and keep us updated, Jake," Olerhy said as he and Tank squatted down to get a closer view of the huge, bloody paw prints.

"Look," Tank said as he pointed at the headless body. "That's Shalur Tufur. I would know that 'forked' Disciple tattoo anywhere!"

Olerhy mumbled, "Damn, the dogs did us a favor killing that scum bag!"

His phone rang. "This is Chief Shanahan. Any concrete leads over there. The media is going bananas over these murders!"

"Killer mutant dogs, Chief!"

After a brief silence, the chief said impatiently, "I want you guys to go over to the 31st Street beach. A 6-year-old Irish girl, Catherine Sullivan, was mauled to death by a school of flesh-eating fish. And she is the daughter of the mayor's nephew. Call me once you check out the scene."

"Will do, Chief!"

"And did you say 'killer mutant dogs', Olerhy?"

CHAPTER SIX

The months zipped past. I started to rely more and more on Chappy as my assistant. I was increasingly amazed at his sponge-like mind; it was if he had the eye of God, because nothing - and I mean nothing - swept passed his perception. But by December a series of strange things started to happen to the animals in the class; hatched newborn chicks were normal, except they hooted like owls; the mice had started growing extra limbs, and their offspring displayed pumped-up bodies and unusual strength. They had three times the muscle mass and strength of their parents. You could even hear the loud thump as they rammed into the cage bars. Yet some of them had bizarrely shaped bodies. Some had three eyes and two tails.

I completed my masters and doctoral work at the University of Illinois in Chicago on the effect of the myostatin gene on inhibiting muscle growth based on experiments in mice and cattle. Then I noticed with astonishment that even the piranhas had grown in size…even their diet had increased significantly. I was baffled by this unusual display until, by sheer accident, I forgot my grade book in class after work; when I went back to get it I saw Chappy injecting a hypodermic needle into a rat's cerebral cortex.

"Chappy, what in the hell are you doing?"

He quickly turned around and peered at me with surprise.

"What's happening, Dr. Hambolin?"

"I guess you better explain that."

"Well, I was just testing a DNA theory of mine on one of your pregnant rats. It's perfectly harmless. I wanted to find out what would happen if you transplanted human neural stem cells into the embryonic brain of a creature. I have discovered that injecting the myostatin gene into the embryo of this mouse," he held it up high by its tail. "I call it *Mighty Mouse;* made it grow 30 percent larger than this one," he picked up a normal mouse in the cage.

"Chappy, you know damn well that I have strict rules about how these animals should be treated. And as I told you before, we don't stray from their diet and I have done research on myostatin proteins, and we still don't know its long-term effects on the body."

"Chill out, Dr. Hambolin, open your mind. The positive thing is that my research might help find a cure and treatment for Muscular Dystrophy, a condition in which the muscles weaken and degrade over time. What I am trying to find is a protein, that instead of turning off a myostatin gene in all of DNA, one that could simply inhibit myostatin. That discovery could help cure degenerative muscular diseases. Sports and body builders will have a new steroid!"

At that moment, it dawned on me that Chappy was probably responsible for the mutant rats, mice, and piranhas.

"Chappy, this could get very serious. This could get both of us in very serious trouble. This is a bioethical issue, so you had better listen closely to what I'm going to say. What if the rat displays human-like behavior? What if they start to think logically and not instinctively? What if, God help us, rats grow to the size of raccoons or small dogs, and start to attack people?!"

"I'm listening, but Dr. Hambolin, what you're saying is nonsense. Our frontal lobe is a bit larger than a rat's. I am shocked you would make such a statement!"

"You are responsible for the weird changes in most of these animals aren't you?"

"I think not!"

"What? I can't think of any other rational means of explaining why everything in this damn room is going berserk."

"Dr. Hambolin, I didn't do any of it, or whatever you're…"

My attention shifted to the floor near Chappy's feet, where a small black box sat. A lizard like tail poked out of it.

"Chappy, what's in the box?"

He nervously peered down at the box. His face twitched spasmodically. He dropped the syringe and the mouse into the cage and quickly picked up the black box, holding as if it were invaluable.

"Chappy what's in the box?" I repeated.

"I'm sorry, but you just wouldn't understand. And you mustn't try. It's a creation of genius. My genius, Dr. Hambolin, will shock the world!"

"Chappy, at least let me try to understand. Just let me look at it. You might have created something that will be destructive. Surely, with your brain, you understand the possibility of creating a deadly transpecie virus.

"When the time is right, Dr. Hambolin, the world will witness my genius. Not until then."

"Well, damn it Chappy, I'll just have to take it!"

I ran toward him. He nervously darted toward the door, grasping the box as if were a football. He ran down the hallway, looking at me furtively. I quickly ran after him, but finally decided to wait until Monday.

- ◊ -

As Chappy walked down the street, he wondered why it took Dr. Hambolin so long to connect him with the mutations in his lab. His eyes then veered toward a piece of cardboard with a picture of Michael Jackson on it. His hands were clasped, and he had sort of an angelic stare toward the sky.

As he clung to the black box, his blood tingled. That's when the *wah wah* sound of an approaching police car's siren made him back pedal to the curb.

"Niggar, didn't you hear the goddamned siren? Huh, boy?"

The doors slammed as two burly White police officers approached him. He glanced at their nametags: Bradigan and Danehy. They were both Irish. They were also well known in the neighborhood as being racists.

"Yeah, I heard it!"

"What do you mean *yeah*, boy? Don't they teach you proper English in school?"

"You realize jaywalking is a fucking crime, boy?" Officer Danehy said.

"My name is Chapworth, not *boy* and not *niggar*!" He became dizzy as his brain felt unhinged from the slap of the cop's hand. The force of it sent him crashing to the sidewalk.

"Niggar, I call you what I want!"

"Brad, let's get out of here," Officer Danehy said. "We're causing too much attention!" A crowd of angry Black people started walking toward the scene.

"Alright boy, we'll be watching you!"

"You alright son?" an elderly woman asked him as she extended her hand to help him up.

"Thanks, I'm alright." He rubbed his sore jaw as he brushed off his clothes and picked up his black box. He thought to himself, *Exodus 21:24-25*:

An eye for an eye, a tooth for a tooth…I know what shift they work.

He got off the main street and walked down an alley. A mangled sign hung crooked on a large door: MOUNT SAINTHOOD BAPTIST CHURCH, REV. H.B. PARSON.

His hand began to sweat. Yet deep within him was an urge to go somewhere and think. As he walked down the alley at back of the church, his ears caught the sound of the reverend's voice.

"Heavenly father thank you for delivering us from the unseen. Because we walk by faith not sight! Amen!"

The congregation moaned. *"Yesss…lord!"*

"Father, we trust your power will guide and protect us from the mean streets of Chicago!"

"Yes Jesus!"

"We know you an almighty God and you can deliver us from the guns, gangs, and dope that lurk around every corner in our neighborhood!"

"Have mercy, Jesus!"

Chappy cynically dismissed the reverend's words as rhetoric. Where was God when his father was shot down for no reason? He walked out of the alley and entered a snack shop where he ordered a hotdog and Coke. He sat down at a nearby table. He had gotten himself into such a nervous frenzy with Dr. Hambolin and the racist cops that he could feel his heart pounding in his chest. He rubbed his swollen temple.

He picked up a newspaper on the table and felt his whole body tremble with astonishment and disbelief as he looked at a photo of a man holding a huge 60-inch-long, 124-pound fish. He read the front-page headline:

5-FOOT LONG FLESH-EATING MUTANT FISH ATTACK CHILDREN AT BEACH!

Chicago- Flesh-eating mutant fish have attacked children at Chicago beaches. Fish with piranha characteristics have also been discovered near Chicago's wastewater treatment plants.

Scientists are trying to determine if chemicals that disrupt DNA are responsible for their voracious appetite for human flesh. University of Chicago biologist James Watlick recently dissected some of the fish.

"This is the first mutation I have seen as a scientist that absolutely terrifies me," said Watlick, 62, a professor at the university's biogenetic lab.

"Not only are these fish equipped with razor sharp teeth, but they have both male and female sex genitalia, which means chemicals are disrupting sexual hormones. To make a long story short, we don't know what is causing the deformities."

Scientists and police have found some evidence that the fish are possibly the result of genetic engineering between red-bellied piranhas and bluegills, a sunfish found close to shore in

Lake Michigan.

"We are all concerned about the safety of our public beaches. This is a first in Chicago's Lake Michigan history," said Jay Townsend, Chicago's Metro Wastewater Reclamation District's governmental officer.

Chappy shoved the newspaper to the other side of the table. He wondered what they had found. Did he leave something at the beach that would implicate him? He reached into his school bag to pull out his notebook and he wrote: *By transforming genetic material of a bluegill, implanting the myostatin protein into the eggs of a female member of the red-bellied piranha, and allowing it to grow…eureka! I have created a mutant killer fish!*

He smiled and quickly glanced around the snack shop. He gazed at the waitress; Phyllis's Rhino-sized ass protruded as she bent down sweeping refuse into a dustpan. She stood up smiling, knowing he was gazing at her *gluteus maximus*. His eyes veered swiftly over the snack shop window and he peered out at the gray, sunless afternoon sky. He longed to be near his girlfriend Bonnie, who was visiting her sick grandmother in Mississippi.

He looked cynically at a group of young high school girls sat at a table adjacent to him, chatting about who would make the cheerleading team. Phyllis slid a plate with hotdog and fries to him.

"Enjoy, Chappy…how is your family doing?"

"They're okay, Phyllis."

He sighed depressively as he bit into his hotdog. He wondered why a teacher of Dr. Hamoblin's stature refused to recognize his genius. He glanced down at the black box as the thing inside it started making a rustling noise like the one the squirrels in biology class did when they were playing. He quickly tore a piece of meat off the hotdog and dropped it into the black box. The rustling abruptly stopped. He opened his notebook and read:

Chapworth's Theory

Ultimately, I want to create an army of transgenic creatures with human brain genes and the myostatin gene inhibitor for super strength and size to fight crime in the Black community. I will use all types of genetically engineered animals to fight my war: cats, rats, monkeys, fish, and even killer pit bulls. Double muscling is a trait previously described in several mammalian species, including cattle and sheep by mutation in MSTN, called in the whippet dog phenotype as 'bully' whippet. I have created two 'bully' pit bulls; Ali and Frazier.

- ◊ -

Chappy glanced out of the window of the old van that he had bought from a junky. He parked it across the street from the police station. He looked at his watch; it was 7:30 p.m. He knew that officers Bradigan and Danehy would be getting off work at eight. He turned around in his seat and patted the bull-sized heads of his monstrous pit bulls, Ali and Frazier. They were the size of Great Danes now, and weighed 250 pounds each. As they licked his hand, he marveled at his genetic creations. His friends called them 'bully pit bulls' and that's why he kept them hidden in an abandoned railroad car near his apartment complex. He thought, *if only Dr. Hambolin knew what I had created in his lab at DuSable High School.* He had successfully injected bitch embryos with MSTN - a myostatin protein that had a tiny mutation of two of the gene's DNA bases, which produced the bully pit bull pups. He had also done this with an army of mice, rats, rabbits, cats, and birds. He hoped one day to have human guinea pigs.

The downside was their voracious appetite. It was becoming difficult to feed them. His solution was that late at night, he would let them loose to roam freely in the parks and alleys to fulfill their appetites with feral cats, coyotes, raccoons, rabbits, and squirrels.

Suddenly, his thoughts vanished as the two officers walked to a car. Bradigan got in the driver's side and Danehy into the passenger seat. It was a silver-grey BMW; it seemed a little too expensive for Bradagan's salary. Earlier Chappy had made a tiny puncture in the rear tire, making sure they would have to eventually get out of the car to fix it before arriving home. They swerved out of the police station parking lot and headed east toward Lake Shore Drive. Bradigan exited the expressway at North Avenue Beach.

The beach was deserted. The waves from Lake Michigan seemed ominous as they blasted the rocks on the shoreline. Seagulls squawked and hovered over them, waiting for discarded food. Dark gray clouds that looked like claws engulfed a full moon. Bradigan parked the car, leaving his emergency blinking lights on. He grabbed a garbage bag with $20,000 of payoff dope money in it and tossed it in the trunk. He grabbed the flashlight and tire jack, and Danehy picked up his spare tire. As Bradigan jacked up the rear of the car, Danehy lit a cigarette. He patted his waist holster for his .24 caliber semiautomatic Beretta, which was loaded with a nine round chrome clip. Danehy nervously peered around the parking area. They were completely alone. He deeply inhaled the smell of rotten fish, and the pungent odor of beach refuse stung his nostrils.

"Brad, you want a cigarette?"

"No, all I got to do is tighten these lugs and we out of here. Can you aim the flashlight over here?" Danehy became edgy as an old van swerved into view. *Probably some college kids making out*, he thought. Bradigan stood up and tossed the jack and flat tire in the trunk.

"Let's get out of here. I need a beer and a steak!"

"I'll second that...."

Both of them looked as the van door opened and two large dogs, silhouetted against a full moon, stood on either side of a boy. The boy slowly walked toward them with a choke leash on the monstrous dogs' necks. Danehy pointed the flashlight at the boy's face and the dogs' luminous demonic eyes gazed at them. The dogs were the size of small lions, with tiger-like stripes on them.

"Remember me!?" Chappy shouted. "The *niggar*? The *boy*? I still feel the pain and sting of that slap from you. You racist SOBs!"

"If you thought that hurt," Bradagan hollered. "*Boy,* you better stop where you at before we blow you and those fuckin' dogs back to the Southside!" A bolt of naked fear tore through the cops' mask of machismo. Chappy and the dogs were less than 20 feet away. Bradagan and Danehy aimed their Berettas at them.

"Attack! Kill the SOBs!" Chappy pointed the wireless transmitter at the dogs.

"Attack!" Chappy commanded as he backpedaled toward the van. The dogs became a blur as their choke chains kicked up a mini-sandstorm, fogging the cops' already dim night vision. Hair bristled on the dogs' backs as they leaped toward them. They fired over and over again.

Both of them catapulted backwards from the impact of the dogs' weight as the bullets tore through them. The dogs mauled them like ravenous wolves; their sharp canines ripped out their jugular veins and carotid arteries. The sand turned red with blood, as the two of them lay dead at the North Avenue Beach. Chappy drove past the carnage. He smiled and continued to drive south on Lake Shore Drive.

CHAPTER SEVEN

The 31st Street beach was buzzing with law enforcement: K-9s, the medical examiner's office, the University of Chicago's Bioresearch department, police helicopters, and the Coast Guard.

"Detective Olerhy? Sam O'Donnel, Channel 7 news -- is it true that the girl was attacked by unknown predator fish?"

The media circus had started. Groups of reporters were starting to encircle detectives Olerhy and Tank. Tank held up his large tree trunk arms, waving back the reporters.

"First, I want you to give this child some respect," he cracked his knuckles on his baseball-sized fist. "You must let us do our job so we can give her grieving parents an explanation for her death."

The reporters backed away nodding. They were intimidated by Tank's 6 foot, 7 inch Alabama DE frame.

"Good work, Tank, I think they got it!" Olerhy said proudly. They slowly walked toward the rectangular yellow-taped crime scene where the girl's body lay. A pristine blue sky with white cumulous clouds blanketed the scorching sun. Seagulls screeched as they circled, like vultures, over the dead girl's body, patiently waiting to scoop down and devour her flesh.

"Detective Olerhy, you might want to see this!" a crime scene investigator said.

It was a plastic evidence bag with a torn sheet of notebook paper inside. Olerhy signed an evidence release form and took it from the crime scene tech.

"Some kind of note in there?" Tank asked curiously. Olerhy held up the plastic bag toward the sun, trying to read the scribble on the paper. He didn't open it because he feared he would contaminate the evidence. He quenched his eyes from the sun's glare. On the right upper corner, *Chapworth's Notes, DuSable High School,* was written.

"Anybody we know?" Tank bellowed out as he pinched his nose from the rotting odor of the mauled remains of young Catherine Sullivan's body.

"Tank, you drive," Olerhy said as he cuffed his nose and mouth, turning around and walking back toward their vehicle.

"Where are we going?"

"DuSable High School!"

"DuSable High School?" Tank said incredulously.

"Yes, we need to question a student by the name of Chapworth."

CHAPTER EIGHT

Chappy rose out of his seat and quickly walked outside the snack shop, waving at some of his classmates. Above him, a large Jumbo jet droned through the morning sky. He stopped at a bus stop on M.L. King Drive. It was hard to hold back the tears from the deaths of Ali and Frazier. Yet their deaths were heroic, because they had killed two racist cops that had gunned down two innocent Black boys and were found not guilty of the crime. A bus snaked into view; he tossed a CTA token into the fare box and walked toward the rear. He sat down as he listened to a radio broadcast:

BREAKING NEWS............LAST NIGHT TWO OFF-DUTY CHICAGO POLICE OFFICERS WERE KILLED BY TWO MONSTROUS DOGS. THE MAULED BODIES OF OFFICER BRADIGAN AND DANEHY WERE FOUND IN THE PARKING AREA OF NORTH AVENUE BEACH.

GOLD COAST DETECTIVES STATE THERE MIGHT BE A LINK BETWEEN THE RECENT ATTACKS OF CHILDREN AT CHICAGO BEACHES BY A NEW SPECIES OF PIRANHA...MORE NEWS AS WE GET IT!

Suddenly, Chappy's whole body shook with terror. He seethed with disbelief. He ran to the front of the bus and screamed.

"Bus driver stop! Damn it let me off!"

He quickly pushed the front door open and jumped off the bus. He started running back toward the snack shop, hoping no one had taken the black box. As he neared the snack shop, he noticed a large crowd of people milling around its windows. He listened to snippets of conversation as they floated through the evening air.

"It's like something out of a monster movie!"

"It just killed those young girls!"

"It snatched Phyllis's head clean off!

"Damn, it looks part ape, human, and lizard combined!"

Phyllis was dead. She had just asked about his family. He became teary-eyed. Sirens bombarded his head. He gazed at the crowd as it milled around the restaurant -- he wondered if it was too late. He knew that the monster's growth rate would increase every hour without being injected with the myostatin blocker. Another problem was that he wasn't sure about the thing's reaction to large crowds. Self-hatred infused him. Chapworth wondered why he had forgotten the box. He wondered if it was a question of fate that actually willed the unleashing of his monster on society. He walked swiftly to the entrance of the snack shop, which was blocked by the police and the large, frantic crowd. A moment later, the sound of crashing glass and a loud animal roar caused the crowd to panic and run, creating uncontrollable chaos. He listened to the police officer on the loud speaker.

"Will you please quietly leave the streets? We are now in a state of emergency. Only you can help us destroy this thing. I repeat, please go to your homes and wait for further instructions."

The crowd scattered with blind panic; each person was concerned with self-preservation. Chappy peered up at the helicopters and down the street at the Army trucks as soldiers leaped onto the ground carrying a vast array of weaponry: grenades, grenade launchers, M-16s, and M-60 machine guns. He wondered if an arsenal could stop the beast. He glanced at the restaurant's shattered windows and again heard the loud beast-like roar that seemingly nullified the power of the Army Reserves' weapons. He wondered if it was a primordial scream, a scream issuing out of anger for having been created in a society that would look upon it with blind hatred. He wondered if he could communicate with the monster. He regretted his brain electrodes were not implanted in the creature.

He quickly scampered toward the entrance of the snack shop. He knew that his life would be completely at the mercy of the monster he had created; still, he thought, his hunch might work. He grabbed the doorknob.

"Stop him! Somebody stop that young man! That thing will kill him!" A police officer shouted.

He entered the dark restaurant. A stream of blind terror enveloped him and he felt an uncontrollable desire to scream. His temples banged like drums and urine trickled down his pant leg from panic and fear. He glanced around the milky-black restaurant. His eyes surveyed the broken equipment and demolished chairs and tables. He peered at the jukebox that looked as though a gigantic foot had stepped on it. There was a busted gas pipe that bellowed out gaseous fumes -- there was a smashed grill plate with greasy French fries upon it; there was a large structural beam of steel, which had been twisted into a tight knot; there was a freezer door that had been virtually torn from its hinges.

He froze when he heard the loud animal roar. He crawled under a table. He listened intensely as loud panting neared the table. The sound of clacking canine-like paws echoed off the floor; it sounded like the slap of a mop as it hit the ground. He glanced down at his hands as they became mushy and wet; they felt as though they had been placed in wet clay. He strained his eyes as he looked at his hands with nausea. He was petrified. Rivulets of sweat oozed from his armpits. The seemingly wet clay was human brains. Were they the brains of Phyllis or the high school girls he saw yesterday? Where were their heads? The stench of rotting carnage engulfed the room. He scooted back underneath the table, cleaning the brain off his hands on his pants. The beast lumbered closer. As he scooted underneath the table, he bumped into a round object. He looked at it. Piteous eyes stared back at him -- dead eyes. He was looking at the decapitated head of Phyllis. He cuffed his mouth and vomited.

How was he going to face this thing when he was so stricken with terror? Chappy's thoughts were shattered as a large shadow loomed directly in front of him on a nearby wall. He peered in the direction of the nightmarish figure. He heard a sighing, rasping sound and then saw his creation. Its huge, reptilian body supported a man-like flat head, which contained two, tiny reddish bulbous eyes. The monster's skin was a nauseating scaly, greenish-blue brown. Its arms and legs were spotted with patches of hair that was clearly African. Its mouth was completely misshapen and chimp-like. Its short neck was muscular and wrinkled like an old vulture. Beads of crystal-like saliva drooled from its wretched lips as it breathed through its ape-shaped nostrils, creating a rasping, hissing sound.

Chappy peered out at the creature. His whole being seemed numb with apprehension and disbelief; yet he knew it was a harsh reality, as harsh and real as the ghetto it was created in; a reality that reflected the capacity of man to tamper with the natural order of nature and create total chaos. His psychic being recoiled at the thought that he had created and placed this wretched *monster* in the midst of the world. He knew the monster was merely an object for the others, haunting their primal consciousness, but at the same time, it existed. It was a wrenching embodiment of man's negation of self.

Chapworth knew that with various types of bacteria, cell division occurs every 24 hours. Maybe that accounted for why the mice died. Maybe during genetic replication periods certain cells died, subsequently weakling the RNA. *Time and space vary for each organism and each individual thing has different growth and death spans, but how can I tie that up with the monster?* He thought. Its huge growth might eventually harm its health. Too much muscle growth could hamper the heart's pumping.

He peered at the monster, standing near the broken shelves like a Stonehenge monolith. He glanced at the blur of light making a silhouette on the creature. It resembled himself. He had injected some of his semen into the embryo of the creature. He noticed that large beads of sweat, like a mist, had started to form on the creature's hair. There was a petrifying odor clinging to it. A bright blue day shone through the ill-fitting slats of the Venetian blinds; bubbles of saliva on the beast's fangs gleamed from slices of light. Chappy smiled as he thought about something Camus, the philosopher, had once wrote:

> *All great deeds and thoughts have a ridiculous beginning. Great works are often born on a street corner or in a restaurant's revolving door.*

He wondered if Camus would consider his *mad* creation a great work of art. His thoughts were like a raging sea tossing him from shore to shore; his giddiness was as though corrosive acid had been poured on an open nerve. He shuddered as the beast sighed. Was it a sigh of sorrow or of capturing him as prey? The monster started to move toward him. It was hideous. It suddenly grabbed the table, lifted it up over him, and tossed it out of the window. Chappy quickly glanced at the electric bulb still containing its delicate filigreed web of wires. He felt like those wires; weak and fragile. He moaned as the monster's too-real reality clinically examined his fear-ridden being. He momentarily closed his eyes and tightened his fists, hoping that he would snap out of this wretched nightmare. A deadening ubiquitous silence rose between them.

Chapworth felt naked as the 12-foot beast towered over him, motionless and breathing with a nauseating sound that evoked a vast, hot void in him. He clenched his teeth to keep them from chattering. He was seized by a ravaging sense of the grotesque being he had created in a world that was already riddled with madness.

He gazed at the beast's vacant eyes, and he knew fate had thrust him into a dead-end situation.

As he looked at the beast, he thought he could have sworn that the thing's gaping mouth was trying to move. He wondered if this frightening experience had driven him to total madness. He shook his head nervously as the monster started to make guttural, human-like sounds. "*Fa... Fa.. Faa..Father!*"

Chapworth slowly rose up from the floor and cautiously walked toward the beast. Was the creature calling him father? At that moment, he heard the police loudspeaker:

"If you are still alive, this is our last warning. Come out! We are going to fire in smoke bombs. This is our last warning. I repeat; we are going to give you one minute."

Chapworth quickly scurried out of the restaurant screaming. "Don't fire! I can control it. Please don't." He broke down in tears, covering his face with his hands.

The sound of bombarding fire nullified his plea. There was total silence. The monster ran out of the smoke-engulfed restaurant, bellowing out an ear-shattering scream.

"Fa...Fa...Father!'

The soldiers and police started firing all their weaponry simultaneously. The monster seemed immune to the constant flow of bullets. It started to knock over cars in a blind panic and animal rage. The police and Army were numb with disbelief. The sheer strength of the beast was amazing. It refused to die. Chapworth started to run toward the beast. It ran with an ape-like gape toward DuSable High School. Chappy thought of the idiots who didn't believe in the will to power and the struggle for existence. He wondered if they'd ever pondered a tree surging toward the sky, or a mammal migrating back to its birthplace.

He glanced at his watch. It was 8:05 p.m. He knew the school would be crowded because Phillips, a hated rival, was playing DuSable for the basketball playoffs. A strange will to end the madness oozed through him. He had only one recurring thought: *the beast had to be destroyed.*

The monster rushed up the school stairs. A mass of students started to run, hollering and screaming.

"What is it?"

"It looks like King Kong and Godzilla put together!"

"It's headed for the gym—hundreds of people are in there!"

At that moment the police, the Army, the National Guard, and the fire department pulled up with sirens blasting. The night sky was a deep black with reddish-orange clouds scratched through it. Chappy quickly ran up the stairs and rushed toward the gym. He knew the beast would instinctively detect the chemical odor of the biology lab on the other side of the gym. The beast had to cross the gym to get to the lab. Chappy ran harder as he thought about the bloody deaths of the students and parents at the game if he didn't stop the beast.

CHAPTER NINE

He walked into the gym and listened. It seemed the basketball spectators thought the beast was a practical joke. They were so enthused by the game they had become collectively blind to anything else. He listened to the large crowd as it roared: "Phillips, go on and ease on down the road! DuSable go ease on down the road!"

Chappy ran toward the beast as it lumbered toward the basketball court. Suddenly, silence engulfed the gym. He glanced at a player who playfully threw a basketball at the beast's head. The beast grabbed the boy, bit off his head, and ripped the boy's body from his spinal cord. It threw the limp, bloody decapitated body into the spectator's stand. The crowd panicked and started jumping to the floor from the bleachers.

Total chaos followed. At that point, the troops burst into the gymnasium and started firing a mother lode of weapons at the beast. The monster began grabbing students and parents at random, snapping spinal cords, snapping off heads, and squashing their limp bodies with its reptilian feet. Chappy noticed that thick drops of congealed blood were clinging to the hair of the beast. The *rattat tat* of the bullets were weakening the creature. Chappy rushed toward the beast as his classmates looked at him as if he were crazy. As he neared it, the creature walked toward him as it tossed a beheaded student's body on the floor. It made a guttural sound.

"Fa...Fa... Father!"

The creature reached for him. Chappy knelt down on the bloody gymnasium floor and cried. *If he had only listened to Dr. Hambolin, everything would've been OK.* The creature fell backward on the floor, dead, as more bullets riveted its body. The gymnasium floor was a river of blood. He heard one cop yell.

"All right that should do it! I wonder where in the hell this *thing* came from. It's like something out of a Hollywood B monster movie." As the cop looked at the dead beast, he glanced at Chappy.

"Say, aren't you the same kid who ran into the restaurant?"

"Yeah. That's me!" Chappy said, kneeling as if praying.

"I see," the police officer said as he kneeled down on one leg and whispered. "Well kid, what do you have to do with this beast?"

"I...I...created it!" Chappy said as a large mixed crowd started milling around the beast.

"You what?"

"I created it...damn it!" Perspiration ran down his neck. He was shaken out of his shock by a hand that had placed itself on his shoulder.

"Chappy, does this have anything to do with that *black box*?" Chappy glanced up at Dr. Hambolin, then stood and ran, jumping on the dead beast and screaming with insanity.

"God told me to do it. God told me my creations would avenge my father's death! All I wanted was revenge for my poor father's senseless death. Not a killing field like this. I am only a tool of God!"

Detective Milton Olerhy tapped the officer on his shoulder as he stood up from talking to Chappy.

"Is that kid Roscoe Chapworth?" He pointed at him jumping insanely on the dead beast.

"Yes, that is him detective. He has lost his mind." He yelled at two rookie cops. "Jeff, you and Jones take the kid to the van and put him in a strait jacket."

"I'm Detective Milton Olerhy and this is my partner, Detective Joe Morgan." He pulled his leather fob containing his shield from his inside coat pocket and showed it to Dr. Hambolin.

"Who are you in reference to this kid and this creature?" Tank asked angrily.

"I'm his biology teacher!"

"Dr. Hambolin, I think you will find this interesting." He gave the evidence bag from the beach to the teacher. He held the plastic bag toward the gymnasium light so he could read the scribbling on the notebook cover. He squinted his eyes from the stadium lights' glare.

"Dr. Hambolin, this is very incriminating evidence," Olerhy said compassionately. "Especially since he was your lab assistant."

"Again, I ask you," Tank said menacingly looking at the bloodbath on the gym floor. "How involved were you with creating this monster?"

"Roscoe Chapworth is a genius. I only recently discovered that he was doing some biological research on DNA and the *myostatin protein* on lab animals. This beast is a product of his demented genius."

"Listen, Dr. Hambolin, I need answers fast. I have a personable interest in this case. Phyllis, the waitress at the Goody Snack Shop, was my niece. The funeral director has got to sew her head back on because of you and that lunatic Chappy," Tank said, as his baseball glove-sized hands grabbed Dr. Hambolin by the collar and shook him savagely. "I have killed nerdy punks likes you for looking at me the wrong way. We need answers!"

Olerhy, more compassionate than Tank, displayed concern.

"Tank, he seems like a reasonable man, let him go. Dr. Hambolin, you play straight with us and we'll play straight with you, okay?"

"I tell you I didn't create the beast!" he said nervously while fixing his collar.

"What about the deaths of those gangbangers in your class that had a run-in with Chappy? They were mauled to death by gigantic dogs!" Tank asked with intimidation.

"I didn't have anything to do with that!"

"What about the black box? I guess you don't know anything about that either?" Olerhy said.

"OK…OK…you don't want to cooperate Dr. Hambolin. That's all right; we will just take you down to the station for questioning. Tank, read him his rights."

Tank withdrew a small card from inside his coat pocket and quickly read off his rights, finishing with, "Is that clear Dr. Hambolin?"

"What's clear is that I haven't done anything, and yes, I want legal counsel."

CHAPTER TEN

As Emiel Hambolin and his lawyer, Ray Bervorsky, entered the courtroom, the bailiff rapped his gavel and shouted, "Order in the court!" The incessant chattering quickly stopped and the remaining spectators scrambled for the few empty seats. The clerk, a small, thin man, glanced at Judge Joseph H. Demberg as he walked with a limp through a door behind his dais and nodded his head. The clerk bellowed out, "Quiet! The court is now in session." Then speedily announced the time, date, and other judicial functions.

Judge Demberg, a huge heavy-set man with penetrating blue eyes, distinguished gray hair and thick glasses, glanced at the court reported and spoke.

"The Circuit Court of Chicago, Illinois, will now hold trial for final duration on the verdict of Dr. Emiel Hambolin on any and all issues relating to the murders and destruction of civic and government property by a mutant creature. Bailiff, have them bring in exhibit A, the monster's corpse, which will serve as the prosecuting attorney's evidence."

The court reporter suddenly screamed with blind terror. Her fingers froze as she looked at the size of the monster. The judge's eyes became bulbous as he looked toward the rear of the courtroom. The spectators nervously looked toward the back of the courtroom as the bailiff walked in front of two security guards, who were breathing hard as they pushed the portable gurney bearing the 12-foot monster beneath the judge's rostrum. The judge gazed at the dead beast as he uttered with authority.

"Quiet please. Must I remind you that this is a courtroom?" He sternly looked around the room as though daring anyone to talk, and then continued.

"I, Judge Joseph H. Demberg, wish to announce that this trial's essential purpose is to reach a final and absolute determination on all the elements involved. The court is subject to judge fairly and impartially on all evidence -- be it verbal, exculpatory, or empirical."

The jurors glanced at the creature and then peered at the judge attentively.

Dr. Hambolin's attorney stood up.

"Question your honor?"

"Yes, Mr. Bervorsky?"

"My client and I have no qualms about the Honorable Judge's non-prejudicial outlook, but without the presence of Roscoe Chapworth at this trial, my client, Dr. Emiel Hambolin, one of this city's most influential and respected teachers, is being inferred as the guilty culprit. And that, your honor, is a catalyst for a prejudicial ruling."

The judge cleared his throat, irritated, and spoke. "It is the purpose of this court to arrive at the truth, and certainly a demented or psychologically disturbed child cannot aid toward reaching fairness and equity." Judge Demberg wiped his brow with his handkerchief.

"But Judge...!

"Enough, Mr. Bevorsky, let's get on with the trial!"

Dr. Hambolin and his wife sadly glanced at Bevorsky and wondered if Emiel would get a fair verdict. Richard Davis, the prosecuting attorney, took the floor.

"I have here..." he waved a number of papers at the jury.

"Exactly 25 civil action suits against Roscoe Chapworth and Dr. Emiel Hambolin, totaling millions of dollars in damage to property and the deaths of innocent adults and students. The creation of this real life *King Kong* has cost Chicago incalculable damage and loss of lives. Judge, without wasting you honor's time, I think the concrete evidence is overwhelmingly obvious that Dr. Emiel Hambolin and his student assistant, Roscoe Chapworth, were wholly conscious of creating this monster!"

"Objection, your Honor, the prosecuting attorney is inferring guilt!"

"Objection overruled, continue Mr. Davis."

"Your honor and the jury, the prosecution presents Exhibit B," prosecuting attorney Davis waved a small black notebook at the spectators. "This is Roscoe Chapworth's diary, which states in explicit detail that Chapworth used the facilities of the DuSable High School biology class, where Dr. Hambolin teaches, in which he also states he was Dr. Hambolin's student lab assistant. He used Dr. Hambolin's high school lab to create the dead beast in our midst. It is virtually impossible for Dr. Hambolin to state that he had nothing to do with this. The diary states in lucid detail his experiments in Dr. Hambolin's class! Considering that, I want Dr. Hambolin to take the stand."

The clerk, standing near a metallic roll-top desk, finished swearing in the witness with customary monotone: "Do you solemnly swear to tell the truth, the whole truth, and nothing but -- so help you God?"

"I do."

"Dr. Hambolin, how long have you been teaching at DuSable High school?"

"Fifteen years."

"How long have you known Roscoe Chapworth?"

"Since September of this school year."

"Dr. Hambolin, did you notice anything unusual about Roscoe?"

"Yes, he struck me as brilliant. He's a child prodigy."

"Was he obviously that much different from other students?"

"Yes, absolutely. He was solving algebra problems at four years old."

"Yet, you admit he seemed perfectly healthy and brilliant?"

"Yes, he was sort of a fluke of nature."

"How do you define 'fluke'?"

"I would define a fluke as a person who has unusual and rare abilities, such as Roscoe demonstrated in biology class."

"But, as I understand it, it is not an abnormality?"

"Correct."

"Dr. Hambolin, will you give me an example of Chapworth's extraordinary brilliance?"

"Well, he was actually doing research on DNA or *deoxyribonucleic* acid and *myostatin* inhibitors at eleven years old, and I think that is sheer genius."

"I see…Dr. Hambolin, will you please explain to the court why a perfectly healthy and brilliant student would change into a mentally disturbed genius while taking your class?"

"Objection your honor, the prosecuting attorney Davis is

implying that my client is the cause of..."

"Objection overruled. The prosecuting attorney may continue."

"Dr. Hambolin, you did state that Roscoe Chapworth seemed perfectly normal, yet brilliant in your class. Is that correct?"

"You must understand that Roscoe Chapworth is a rarity, one of a kind, a genius in the classical sense. He's a genius that came from the most wretched and largest subsidized housing project in America, the Robert Taylor Homes in Chicago. He proves a genius can be born in poverty - to name a few, Einstein worked in a patent office, and George Washington Carver was born a slave, but discovered 400 patents for the peanut. The philosopher Spinoza was a lens cutter. The Croatian electrical genius Nikola Tesla was a ditch digger before he worked for Thomas Edison. We can add Roscoe Chapworth to that list. But the tragedy, I think, is when I made him my classroom lab assistant, I failed to realize that he was a mentally sick child. He's a very psychologically disturbed boy that could never get over the blood that splashed on him when a gang member gunned down his father when he was young. Tragically, I realized it too late."

"Dr. Hambolin, to the best of your knowledge, approximately when did Chapworth start showing signs of being mentally ill?"

"Maybe in late March."

"What was it that you noticed?"

"Well, it was just before that monster rampage."

"How long ago?"

"Maybe three months ago."

"And how did you see these signs?"

"It happened by sheer accident. You see, I had forgotten my grade book in class, so I went back to get it and I saw Chapworth standing over one of the mice cages. He was holding a syringe with blood dripping out of it."

"How did he react?"

"He was very cool about it."

"Cool?"

"I mean nonchalant. Not frantic."

"And you?"

"I was mad and frantic as hell. I have specific instructions on how the animals in my biology class should be treated and fed. But most importantly, that incident helped me get everything into perspective. I understood, then, what accounted for the bizarre physical changes of the animals."

"Like what?"

"A couple of guinea pigs were born as two-headed Cyclops. But thankfully they died a day after birth. The newborn mice had grown the size of alley rats. After examining Chapworth's syringe, I found it contained a *myostatin* inhibitor, which can increase muscle and strength growth."

"Dr. Hambolin, after seeing these mutations in your class, why didn't you contact the principal Jack Bradshaw? After all, it was *you* who said it was impossible for Roscoe Chapworth to be as smart as his IQ test had shown, wasn't it?"

"I didn't contact Jack because I thought I could reason with Chapworth. I didn't want him to be punished for being a genius. And yes, when I was first shown his IQ test I couldn't believe it, especially considering the environment he was raised in." A large number of spectators started chattering incessantly.

"Order in the court!" snarled Judge Demberg. "Any further bickering and someone will be held for contempt!"

"Dr. Hambolin, you were aware of the strange occurrences in your biology class prior to the murder of Shalur Tufor, who was found in an alley with his head cut off, along with his beheaded friends, MoonDay-G, Renegade, Cochise, Wack, and Nojo?"

"Well…yes."

"And you were well aware of the mutations in your biology class?"

"Indeed I was."

"Well, Dr. Hambolin, for Christ's sake, will you please tell the court why you didn't tell the FBI and the detectives when they contacted you about finding Chapworth's notebook at the 31st Street beach, about his experiments in growth mutations? You read the newspaper, listen to the radio, and watch TV like the rest of us. Didn't you at least wonder about the number of child deaths in Lake Michigan, which was attributed to mutant piranha-like fish? What about the deaths of two of Chicago's finest police officers, Bradagan and Danehy, who were mauled to death by two mutant pit bulls at North Avenue beach? It seems to me you were more curious about Chapworth's *experiments* than the possible consequences of them."

"I was trying to work out if in fact those deaths were attributed to him. I just waited too long."

"*Wait*! Dr. Hambolin, surely a biology teacher like yourself understands the consequences of time with a deadly disease, like cancer. If you wait too long for medical help, you die. Yet you waited. Why?"

"It's not like you think. I just didn't realize the extent of Chapworth's experiments."

Gloria Hambolin, his wife, frowned and whispered worriedly to Jack Bradshaw. "Jack, the way that attorney is twisting words and everything against Emiel, I doubt Perry Mason could get him out of this."

"Things do look rather bleak. I just hate that Emiel was so secretive about all this. He could have consulted me. And that fuckin' lawyer is trying to use a telephone conversation against Emiel -- one I had with Emiel that my secretary overheard. Emiel should not have been so naïve about this." Their attention shifted back to the trial.

"Dr. Hambolin, in closing a final question: Did you collaborate with Roscoe Chapworth in the creation of this beast?"

"No, I absolutely did not!"

Judge Demberg inhaled a deep breath, then spoke. "The court, over a period of three months, has heard all the relevant and pertinent facts for this case. Does the defendant's counsel, Mr. Bervorsky, choose to bring forward any witnesses or material that will help the jurors reach a verdict on this case?"

"No further questioning Your Honor, I rest my case." A bridge of silence engulfed the courtroom like a dense fog.

"Since the defendant counsel rest his case, the court will now recess for deliberation by the jury on the guilt or non-guilt of Emiel Hambolin. Court is recessed until 1 o'clock."

- ◊ -

I was found guilty and sentenced to three years at the treacherous Menard Penitentiary down state, along with the suspension of my teaching certificate. Roscoe Chapworth had a severe nervous breakdown and is confined to Bellevue, a downstate sanitarium. You may ask why I am still so full of depression. I have lost everything; my 20-year teaching career has been abolished. I have lost my home. I'm divorced, homeless, and have a bad liver from drinking. The answer to the cause of my misery: a student by the name of Roscoe Chapworth. Not a day goes by in my wretched life that I don't think of his evil genius with rage and regret.

Darwin's Ghetto

John Sibley

HEX

Rufus Braswell stood there while inhaling the putrid odor that seemed to creep from the decaying metal and plaster. As he gazed at the gutted building it reminded him how all things seem to fall into the inescapable jaws of entropy. And yet, even though the large building was now nothing but the smoldering ruins of a fire, it still seemed to generate a force of its own. It was a force that transcended the material world; a force that existed outside of a three-dimensional universe.

The large brick Victorian six- flat that his grandmother once lived in was a place he would never forget; it seemed much larger than it actually was. It seemed to contain an aura of mystery and exhumed a scent of ghostly gloom. The building was shrouded with a history of unusual occurrences. Many of the old-timers that lived on the block used to talk about it being *haunted,* with *spooks* and *shadowy things* that would creep around the old building at night.

Rufus peered up at the deathly gray sky as large black crows *caw cawed* as they glided around the large conical roof, which would fit perfectly into one of Poe's most ghastly tales. He stood hypnotized as his gaze again focused on the old building's remains, as if he were at a cemetery. His mind flashed back to where he could actually *hear* and *see* his childhood memories. He could hear with crystal clarity Grandma Malone's coarse voice saying to his mother on the phone,

"I tell you Mattie Bee, Rufus can see things. You told me he was born with a veil over his eyes, right?" (He smiled as he thought about how she associated at birth the covering of his eyes by the placenta, as a psychic *veil,* which could enable him to see entities in the spirit world). *Ziiiing* went the metallic sound of her snuff as she spit with the aim of a missile and it splashed into a metal pail, dramatizing the conversation with his mother.

Rufus stood there watching his grandmother as she picked collard greens and spat snuff into her rusty pail.

"Grandma, I don't wanna go home!" He said mournfully. She spat and cackled, "Mattie Bee, you hear him? Rufus said he don't want to leave me. Don't want to go home -- loooord de beee. 'Um telling you that boy is something else... haha, actin' grown already and he only 8 years old!"

Rufus looked at his Grandma Malone. She was a tall, light-skinned woman who was part Cherokee; her face portrayed large, bulging cheekbones, a chiseled mouth and nose, thick lips and short, silvery gray hair. She was a mulatto - a French aristocrat raped her mother. She was born and raised on a sharecropper's farm in Alexandria, Louisiana, a place known for its belief in the supernatural. It was a town where she was weaned on a daily dosage of hoodoo magic and the shadowy world. She used to make the hair on his neck rise when she told him ghostly tales of angry restless spirits of slaughtered Indians and lynched slaves, which she said roamed the countryside at night looking for revenge, whom the local folks called *spooks*.

"It's the little people, grandma!" Rufus would shout.

Rufus ran into the living room hoping to see them again; they were small, colorfully dressed gnomish-like creatures that danced around in a circle as if performing some ancient burial ritual. His young mind was more puzzled than scared. He wondered why they only revealed themselves to him. Was that why his mother said he was born with a veil over his face? He scurried back into the kitchen and grabbed his grandma's apron as she continued to pick collard greens and talk to his mother. "Grandma, they are here.

HEX

C'mon grandma, I see them!" He pulled on her apron as she patted his hand.

"Mattie Bee, gonna let you go because your son is seeing things again. Rufus say some spooks in the living room. Talk to you later."

She walked toward the stove and dropped some ham hocks into the greens and then she accidentally knocked a half-cut chicken onto the floor. Rufus looked at it and jumped back. He saw its glistening entrails sprawl on her shiny wooden floor as blood spilled from it. He peered at the yellow rigid claws as they jolted skyward as though defiantly renouncing death. Then he noticed a black bag next to the chicken. He picked it up and chicken bones, feathers, peanut shells, garlic bulbs, a tiny vial of blood, and chicken feet fell to the floor. He did not realize it was her "*Hex Bag*" that she used to ward off evil spirits. She stooped down, putting the items back into the bag.

"Rufus, don't mess with my black bag. It keeps evil spirits outta here!"

They started walking down the long hallway toward the living room when she saw something move from behind the front room couch. But it was nothing but the flickering shadow from a large moth that had frightened her. She gasped with relief while patting her heart. Suddenly, her cat Snowball scampered from under a table with its hair bristling on its back and its large green luminous eyes shining brightly. It ran out of the living room and down the hallway. At that instant, she heard a large glass crash on the living room floor.

"Grandma, its them little people!"

She wondered *what he meant by 'little people'. Did he mean demons or some kind of ghost? Spooks? Goblins? On the other hand, was it just his imaginative 8-year-old mind?* As she stood there, patting Rufus on the head, a blast of cold air stirred the curtains, creating whirling figurative shadows on the walls. Her dead husband, Matt's, rocking chair suddenly started rocking and squeaking. She bellowed out fearfully.

"Is that you in there Matt? If it's you, go back and leave us alone!" Lightning and the roar of thunder sent chills down her spine. The pitter-patter of raindrops echoed from the thunderstorm and rattled the windows. Uncle Miles's dog, Pabst (named after the beer), started to howl mournfully. She prayed.

"*As I walk through the valley of death, I will fear no evil for thou are with me!*"

"Grandma, there they are, see 'em?"

She strained her old eyes as they scanned the living room. Pabst started barking viciously at the couch. Then suddenly she saw them: small, dark, furry, lizard-tail shadows. She stood frozen in her tracks as they scurried under the couch. What were they? She knew her old eyes were not playing tricks on her because both of them had now seen them "little people." Rufus was right and she was petrified. Suddenly, there was the *thump, thump, thump* sound of someone knocking on the kitchen door. She picked up Rufus and ran back to open it.

"Who is it?" she moaned.

"It's me Ma. What's wrong?"

Uncle Miles painfully slumbered into the apartment with bloody scratches on his face and blotches of dried blood on the guitar case he clutched, it as if it were a part of him.

"My Lord, you been in a fight, boy?"

"No big thing, ma, I'm too old for fighting."

"We saw the little people Uncle Miles. Grandma did, too."

HEX

"What's wrong with your face Miles? You been fighting again with Mary Lee?"

"It's not me Ma. Why that crazy woman tried to tear up my guitar. I love Maybelline more than I love any woman! B.B. King got Lucille. I got Maybelline."

"Miles, I have told you over and over again that the woman is a Voodoo queen. She is a mambo; a high priest of Voodoo worship. Stay away from her and her mother. If you hurt her daughter, she will put a hex on you and me. Mary Lee was born under a bad sign, just like her mother. It's in her blood. You tell me why every man that deals with her daughter ends up dead, sick, or missing?"

Uncle Miles wiped blood from his scratched brow as he walked down the long, cavernous hallway toward his bedroom. Uncle Miles was a bluesman. His father, Matt Malone, had taught him in his youth, when he visited him in Jackson, Mississippi, to play the guitar. He did so by stretching the taut wire from an old straw broom on a wall and nailing each end, and then rubbing a bottle over the wire to create the tonal effects of guitar notes. Miles's Chicago blues fans said that the sounds from his guitar conjured up images of the dark spiritual world. By the notes he strummed on his guitar, he believed could *evoke* spirits from ancient African rituals. Blind Tom, a Nigerian Conga player, once told him that the *pulse*, the *rhythm*, even the syncopation of his music, reminded him of the religious Ibo dance back in Nigeria.

He started to tremble as he crept down the hallway. Aches and pains from his fight with Mary Lee ravaged his body. Maybe he should have listened to his mother a long time ago, to stay away from her. To stay away from the evil gray eyes that were now ashes. They were dead, yet staring at him. He bit down on his lower lip so hard, blood trickled down the side of his mouth.

He stopped walking when he thought he heard footsteps behind him. Suddenly, a blast of Mary Lee's perfume wafted under his nose. He blinked his eyes repeatedly, trying to block out the wretched horror of her dead, beaten body popping, crackling, and glowing ghastly flames from the scorching basement furnace where he had stuffed her small body. He had hit her in the mouth and she fell, hitting her head on the radiator and breaking her neck. It was a freakish accident, but who would believe him? That's why he had to destroy the body. He walked into his bedroom and slammed the door.

Bam, bam, bam! His mother knocked on his door.

"Miles, will you open the door? I'm worried about you." A cluster of thoughts bounced in her head: Was he sick? Suicidal? Drunk? Her old, knotted hands shook with tension as she grabbed a key chain from around her neck and opened her son's squeaking bedroom door. She stood there, petrified with disbelief as she gazed at Miles's empty guitar case on the bed next to him. He lay on the bed as if crucified. Her old heart pounded with fear. She moaned.

"Miles, now don't you play games on your old mother, don't be playing possum!" She walked over to him and heard him snoring.

"Where is Uncle Miles's guitar, grandma?" Rufus asked as they walked out of his bedroom and she shut his door. She shook her head with grief. She realized that Miles would never leave his beloved guitar - never! He would leave his woman, his job, his money. But he would never leave his sacred Maybelline. He slept with it, ate with it. And there were tales that he couldn't have sex without it near him.

"Why did Uncle Miles leave his guitar grandma?"

"Shoooosh Rufus, you giving me a headache! C'mon, let me cook some dinner for us." She thought Miles must have been really tired. Suddenly there was a loud knock and she could hear

Pabst barking at the kitchen door. She quickly walked down the hallway. She whispered as she quieted Pabst and gripped the doorknob. They banged on the door again and again. She thought *whoever they are, they not neighbors.* Pabst barked and growled nervously. He was a mean brown and white mixed poodle with a vicious temper.

"Who is it?" she asked angrily.

"Are you the mother of Miles Malone, the bluesman?" a nasal voice called out from behind the locked door.

"Yes, that be her."

"Well, could we speak to you please?"

"Who're you?" she asked nervously.

"The police." The mortise lock latch clicked and the door screeched open with the chain still attached to the upper lock. She looked at a detective's fob as he held it up for her to see from the cracked door. She grabbed the dog, putting him in the bathroom before opening the door.

"Good morning ma'am, I'm Detective Milton Olerhy, and this is my partner detective, Joe 'Tank' Morgan. And what's your name young man?" the Irish detective asked as he patted the boy on his head.

"Rufus, Rufus Braswell, and me and grandma saw little people!" the boy said emphatically.

"Little people, ma'am?" Olerhy and Tank whispered.

"He can see *things*. He was born with a veil over his eyes!"

"A veil Miss Malone?" Detective Olerhy said.

"It's essentially when the placenta is over the eyes at birth. My mother believes that too," Tank said.

"No. You say placenta in the North, but we say *veil* in the South detective Olerhy." She glanced at them up and down. She had seen them in the neighborhood before. She had heard that they only handled homicides. She smelled trouble. "Come on in. How about some coffee, gentlemen?"

"No thanks, Miss Malone! I've been a Miles Malone fan for years, since I was a kid back in the 1950s when my father used to take me to Maxwell Street to listen to him! The tone he got out of the guitar he called Maybelline, the way he shook his left wrist, the way he squeezed the strings," Tank said, as if he had known her for years. "Miles has got to be in his late 50s now right?"

"He's 55!" she snapped. Tank drummed his fingers on the tabletop as the smell of hot pork chops wafted passed his nose.

"Miss Malone, Tank here is not his only fan. Why, I have all his CDs. Man can that guy play the blues. He's in the same league as Howlin' Wolf, Muddy Waters, and BB King! I remember one time on 12th and Halsted -- back then they called it *Jewtown* -- I seen him flip it, kick it, and pluck his guitar with his teeth. The guy is a genius!" Detective Olerhy said with glee.

"No doubt about that. It's in his blood; his father played a guitar with a small band in the Mississippi Delta years ago." She sat down nervously in her kitchen chair, realizing the chitchat was just a warm up before the shit hit the fan. She knew they were just being polite and friendly before asking her about the serious stuff. She already knew it had something to do with Miles. She smiled momentarily as the Irish cop looked to her, more like a gay neighborhood Catholic priest than a detective, as he as he spoke;

"Miss Malone, I only regret that we aren't here on a more festive note. Tank and I respect Miles as a great bluesman. Like we said earlier, the man is a legend, but unfortunately, the gifted can make mistakes. Make bad choices. That's why we have a warrant for his arrest."

"What for? Miles isn't violent. What in God's name happened? I know my son ain't done nothing wrong!" she said with grave trepidation, and tears started to flow down her cheeks. A dog howled from a distant alley. Pabst started to growl from the bathroom as a fly buzzed around her face.

"What's wrong grandma?" Rufus asked with concern as he rubbed her arm.

"Just be quiet boy, old grandma going to be alright. Now what you trying to say about my son? What in Jesus name are you trying to blame him for?"

"Miss Malone," Tank cleared his throat, bracing for her reaction. "Miles will be arrested for the murder of Mary Lee Laveeza, his girlfriend. The janitor found her burnt remains in the basement furnace in her building this morning."

"How you know Miles did it?"

"We found the saw," Olerhy said. "He dismembered her. His bloody fingerprints were all over her apartment. They had a violent fight because her apartment is in ruins. We can pretty much trace the movement of her body all the way to the basement furnace. His bloody guitar is still on her bed! His Caddy is still parked at Mary Lee's apartment building."

Grandma Malone looked down nervously at Rufus, but he did not seem to have listened to what the detectives had said, too interested in watching the fly creep along the hardened floor. He sensed his grandma watching him.

"What about the little people grandma?" Rufus asked.

"You sure that boy ain't slow Miss Malone?" Tank snickered.

"You know how wild children's imaginations at his age are Tank," Olerhy snapped, winking slyly, agreeing with Tank.

"We would like to look in Miles's room. Is that okay, Miss Malone?" Tank asked as he held an arrest warrant for her to look at. Both of them scooted their chairs back and stood up. She rose and started to walk down the hallway toward his room, crying and moaning.

"Don't cry grandma!" Rufus said.

She mumbled to herself as she walked down the hallway, "Why you cause these problems for your old mother?"

As they neared his door, they heard the sound of his guitar.

"He must be playing a CD; his guitar is at Mary's apartment," Tank said.

Detective Olerhy and Tank pulled out their guns as they banged on the door.

"Miles, this is the police. Open the door; we want to talk to you!" Tank said. "Don't force me to use my old Chicago Bear linebacker skills to knock this door down!"

"Miles, open the door before they tear it down, son!" she said apprehensively.

"Miles, if the door ain't open at the count of three, we're going to break it down!"

"One!" Tank said angrily.

"Miles, open the door for your mother, son. You know I got high blood pressure!"

"Two!"

"Uncle Miles, open the door!" Rufus screamed.

"Three!"

"Lord have mercy on your soul Miles!" she hollered.

Boom!

Detective Olerhy and Tank slammed the door down and stared up at his swinging body. Olerhy shook his head with amazement, because it was like looking at a condemned man hanging from the gallows.

"Miles… my Miles done killed his self? Oh Lord, have mercy on my soul. Why Miles? Why?" Grandma Malone wailed. Tank put his arm around her shoulder compassionately and grabbed Rufus's hand, swiftly taking them out of the room and back into the kitchen.

Olerhy noticed how Miles's eyes bulged with fear. His face was contorted with pain. Somehow, his wrists were bound by rope behind him. Someone or *something* had hoisted him up to a heating pipe and put a noose around his neck. Whoever it was then dropped him, dislocating his shoulder and breaking his neck. Dried feces and urine soaked his socks and shoes. He couldn't understand how Miles could have tied that pipe around that ten-foot ceiling without standing on anything.

As Olerhy walked toward an open window he stooped down, looking at feathers, chicken feet, dried blood, and peanut shells underneath his body, which hovered dead center above a five-star pentacle circle drawn in a powdery blue chalk. White roses and petals were also on the floor. Tank walked back in the room and stooped down next to him. He picked up one of the white roses and smelled it.

"It's fresh, as if it was just picked. Must be some kind of occult ritual, huh?"

"No way," Olerhy said. "He couldn't possibly have hung himself. It's impossible. Someone or *something* had to hoist him up there, tie his hands behind his back, and put the noose around his neck." They both gazed up at his dangling body.

"I guest this eliminates any suspects. His mother is too old to lift a 200-pound man," Tank joked.

"Morgan! Respect the dead... please?"

Olerhy walked over to an open windowsill. A wind blasted through, ruffling the small rose petals on the floor. One fell near Tank's shoes. He picked it up and again inhaled its aroma.

"Incredibly fresh. I have never seen a suicide scene like this."

"Why would white rose petals be on the windowsill?" Olerhy stuck his head out of the window. A thin wind ruffled the curtains as he leaned out. Suddenly, thunderstorm clouds started rumbling over the dark sorrowful sky. Flashes of lightning carved the cumulous clouds. Black birds flew overhead, cawing and flying past a full moon. Only six floors down dogs started to bark and howl piteously at Olerhy, as if something unholy were near. Suddenly, Miss Malone ran back into the room crying as she gazed at her hanging son, when she noticed the peanut shells, feathers, and the five-star circle underneath her son's body. She bent down, holding her titanium hip. She moaned as she picked up a white rose from inside the blue chalk circle.

"I know who killed my son!"

"Who, Miss Malone?" Detective Olerhy said as a dog in an alley howled.

"Mama Laveeza and her demons put a *hex* on him!"

"Who is Mama Laveeza, Miss Malone? And what is a hex?" Tank said as he pulled a pen and notebook from inside his coat pocket.

"A hex is an evil spell; a person who practices witchcraft. Mary Lee's mother is a Haitian Voodoo priestess. She's a witch, a sorceress of the highest order. Only she could kill my son." She stooped down and picked up one of the roses, pointing it at them.

"With this poisonous Christmas white rose, which is the one used in powerful spells by mambos, witches, and sorcerers that makes them invisible, she and her demons *killed* my son!"

"Miss Malone, we already talked to Betty Leveeza after she verified her daughter's dental records with her remains. There's no way she could have come over here and hanged Miles! Even though I'm sure she would had liked to!"

"You are right, Detective Olerhy, she didn't kill him. Her magic and demons did!"

"Miss Malone, we have no choice but to write your son's death as a suicide. How he hanged himself, we don't know. But that's the only rational conclusion we can come to." Tank Morgan nodded his head in agreement.

- ◊ -

John Sibley

One week later

Madison and Pulaski

Chicago, Illinois

Across town, on the west side of Chicago, Lawndale was one of the poorest neighborhoods in the city. A neighborhood that resembled the slums of Haiti, Calcutta, India, and the barrios in South America; it's a neighborhood that was a dumping ground for the homeless, vagabonds, winos, addicts, hustlers, pimps, ex-cons, and the physically and mentally impaired. A wooden sign swung on the window of a dingy storefront, written with a blood red marker:

Mama Laveeza

Voodoo Priestess

Read palms, lottery numbers, incense candles

773-419-1968

Detective Milton Olerhy knocked on a wooden door with white peeling paint as he stepped on garlic bulbs, inhaling their pungent odor. The sky was milky black with streaks of crimson slicing through dark cumulous clouds. *It would make a great backup for a horror movie,* he thought. The lock grated and the door screeched open as a frail middle-aged woman with albino skin as white as bone and gray eyes that reminded him of an alpha she-wolf looked out. Mama Laveeza had rope-thick dreadlocks, which drooped around her neck and shoulders like vipers. She looked like a Black Medusa whose glance could turn men into stone. She peered at Olerhy and his partner, Tank.

"Look Olerhy," Tank said. "Done heard enough about spooks, Voodoo and hexes for one day," he said as he took a cigarette out of a packet. "I'll take a smoke while you talk to her!"

"Okay Tank, this shouldn't take long."

Neon lights from Madison Street shone through the dirty blinds and flickered across her face like film celluloid. Her stone alabaster face, which looked haggard and beaten, took on a demonic gleam as pastel blue, orange, and pale yellow light reflected on her parchment-white skin. A long skeletal finger on her knobby hand, with long blood-red-dotted, cerulean blue fingernails, gestured for him to come inside. Olerhy walked in and the door slammed shut behind him.

He felt like he had entered an Egyptian tomb, as though some malicious force was watching his every move. He patted his 9mm pistol confidently as he passed an altar in a candlelit room -- a round table draped with a red silk cloth and a figure of a black Virgin Mary on top. He remembered an old Latin phrase his mother use to say when his father came home in a drunken stupor:

Libera me, Domine...

God have mercy on me.

Olerhy cringed as she smiled, revealing pale, vampire-like teeth. Her slanted wolf-gray eyes were shaped like almonds. A black and gold shawl, with flakes of gold and silver embedded in it, hung from her shoulders.

"I am still mourning my precious Mary Lee's death detective. Can you be brief, sir?" she said with a Creole accent.

"We found Miles Malone's body hanging in his bedroom last week at his mother's apartment. I'm sure you heard about it."

An evening wind rustled through a window and made the curtains snap and pop. Dogs started to howl piteously in an ally. A full moon crisscrossed the blinds. The smell of incense and roses floated in the air. He looked at her, shuffling his feet as he crushed a white rose. It was the same type of rose that was in Miles's bedroom. He could see the faint glow of candles in a backroom and heard voices and the slap of cards on a table. She smiled a satanic smile.

"Praise Pa Pa Legba. Praise Damballa. Praise Witeh Serogah. They have revenged my daughter's death!"

"Do you have any ideas about his death?"

"Detective, you are not listening to me. I just told you who caused his death!" She shut her eyes and balled her fist, gazing toward the ceiling and whispered.

"Detective Olerhy, there are forces in the universe that we have absolutely no control of except with magic, and that is what killed Miles Malone. My magic. Black magic!"

The smell of garbage, mildewed furniture and old clothes wafted past his nose. He looked around the shop at the myriad of objects: bottles filled with a snot-green liquid with floating spiders, snakes, and lizard parts inside; damaged Persian rugs; black velvet paintings of tigers; lacquered vases and bowls laced with fake gold copper and silver; a table with love oils; lottery books; a jar with hoodoo dust labeled on it, and another labeled "mojo" cream. He glanced at a sign that read:

HEX BE GONE

Incense powder or sticks

Help block and kill any HEX

Help stop bad luck in gambling

Turn back evil

Next to it, he read another sign:

VOODOO DOLL

Easy to use, not harmful

HEX

No. D489 Male doll... $8.

No. D589 Female doll... $8.

Mama Laveeza pointed a boney finger at a nearby table. He followed her, squeezing down an aisle cluttered with used furniture. Olerhy slowed down as he passed a Plexiglas box with dozens of hissing snakes whose heads poked at the glass. He wondered: *Where they real or some holographic toy?* She pointed down at a vanity table with twisted knotted legs; on top of it was a cracked Miles Malone album cover.

Adjacent to the album cover was a tiny mummy with a cat's head wrapped around wood. Olerhy started to reach for the wooden mummy sarcophagus.

"Don't touch that!" she screamed. Olerhy felt something brush against his leg. He gazed down at a huge black cat with lime-green eyes. He brushed his hand against his holstered 9mm Heckler & Koch handgun -- he was getting nervous. The place was becoming creepy. Suddenly, a shadow-caped silhouette floated on the cracked walls.

Mama Laveeza was known throughout the Westside as a Voodoo queen. Her shop sold vast quantities of Voodoo portions and charms to be used for good or evil, but they would only work after paying a small fee to her, who was well versed in Voodoo lore. Mama Laveeza was not only called a Voodoo queen, but a conjuror, root doctor, shaman, and witch doctor. Among her most potent fetishes was High John the Conqueror Root (which had to be gathered before September to be effective). High John was combined with her magic shawl wrapped around her shoulders, which she said was sent to America by the emperor of China in 1830, and made her a powerful Voodoo queen.

"Detective, if you ever become impotent, I have a special love portion made from a cat's testicles, and I place them in a chamois sack and sew the top together and you just tie it to you genitals. Your impotence will disappear in a week."

"I'll stick with zinc," Olerhy said matter-of-factly.

"You name it detective; I have a remedy for it. Considering your Irish heritage, Catholics often nail a saint's picture over their doors to ward off an evil curse or hex. Did you know that human hair is commonly used in creating death portions or harmful medicines? That garlic is believed to turn away spirits of the dead and to protect you from evil. That a broom hung over a door is said to keep sickness and disease away from home?"

"No I didn't, but I didn't come here for a lecture on black magic. Again I ask, do you…"

"Over there is your answer," she pointed, picking up the mummified cat he wanted to touch.

"This is the mummified cat-headed goddess *Bast*," She held it up toward the ceiling light, "that Howard Carter stole from the tomb of Tutankhamen when he entered the chamber on November 26, 1922. It was lost until 1987 when it showed up in the private collection of the wealthy Mr. De Guiehand's family in Louisiana. When he died a mysterious death, some say because of the mummy's curse, a black servant by the name of Elijah Lagor stole it and it was never seen again until after his death, where his sister sold it to Marie Leveau, my great great grandmother, who was born and raised in New Orleans in 1827. It was then given to her daughter, Maria Lavea, who dominated Voodoo in New Orleans for forty years. She had a shop on Perdido Street. I studied Voodoo under Maria, and she gave it to me on her deathbed. Some attribute the death of Lincoln and Kennedy to it. Legend has it that anyone that touches it or harms its owner, or that has harmed the owner's family, will die a hideous death. After killing my daughter, Miles came up from the basement and must have touched it to prove he did not believe its power. If you look hard," she pointed her fingernail at the cat's head, "you can see drops of blood on it." Detective Olerhy shook his head with frustration.

"Look Mama Laveeza, you're wasting my time and yours. I don't believe in ghosts. I am not superstitious. I don't believe in *hocus-pocus*. As a Catholic, it's hard for me to believe that Jesus resurrected from the dead! I believe in the facts," he looked at his watch. "It's getting late. Just a few more questions and --"

"So you don't believe in ghosts, you don't believe in spirits, you don't believe Jesus rose from the dead, and you don't believe in magic! Would you believe that when Jimi Hendrix played 'Electric Lady' the beat was exactly like the Voodoo ceremonies in Ghana? Jimi used Voodoo in his music to guide his audience like a houngan. He even danced across the stage dressed like a houngan with his clothes, jewelry, feathers, hat, and scarf. Detective, I am sure you have listened to the classic 'Voodoo Chile,' huh?"

"Yes, it's one of my favorites. His harmonics genius was unheard of at the time, a genius like Miles Malone, which is why I am here. In case you have forgotten!"

"Miles was not a believer like you. His music was more religious-based. Pentecostal!"

"Will you please give me a break on this mumbo jumbo? Jimi Hendrix was not into Voodoo worship, and I don't believe in nothing but concrete reality, which is why Miles Malone's death is so puzzling."

Someone banged on the door, loudly and angrily. A man's voice shouted from behind it.

"You said this $50 Lucky Gambler's necklace would help me win the lottery!" A middle-aged man's voice bellowed. "You said tonight's winning number would be a triple! I just spent my baby mama's last money on this necklace and the triple 666 like you told me. You conned me Mama Laveeza and I want my money back!"

She hobbled to the door unlocked the bottom, but left the chain on the top. She cracked the door open and whispered,

"Mr. Taylor, play 666 all week and your reward will be bountiful. An nigguh, don't you ever *bam* on my fuckin' door again or I will put a hex your sorry black ass!" She walked back over to Detective Olerhy with the mummified cat in her hand.

"So, you are a doubting Thomas detective?"

"Look, you're wasting my time," Olerhy said again. He glanced at his watch. "I didn't come over here to discuss ghosts and hoodoo, but to get your take on Miles Malone's suicide!"

"I'm going to let you in on a secret," she said pointing to his chest. "You ever heard of ghost particles?"

"No, what has that got to do with Miles's death?"

"*Shooosh!*" She put her long fingernail to his mouth. "The physicist Wolfgang Pauli proposed that a new particle -- which is flowing through us at this very moment -- cannot be detected, as it has no electrical charge, no mass which is called a *Neutrino*, which means 'little neutral one' in Italian."

"Again, what has that got to with Miles Malone's death?" he said, scratching his head in confusion.

"Listen to me Detective Olerhy -- don't let my dreadlocks and the way I talk and live fool you. In high school I won a four-year academic scholarship to the University of Illinois in Urbana to major in physics, but I rejected it because they don't teach magic and alchemy like Maria Lavea taught me in her shop in New Orleans."

"Alchemy?"

"Yes detective, a form of chemistry studied in the Middle Ages which used magic to make base metals into gold and to discover immortality."

"Interesting... but again, let's get back to Miles's death."

"Listen closely detective. Again, here is your answer. When you look at boiling water, you are normally witnessing the random direction of jiggling vibrating atoms, but what if you could control the atoms and make them vibrate in unison, and suppose this was in an upward direction. Is this what happened in the biblical account of the Red Sea parting for Moses and his people? Or did this happen on the Sea of Galilee where the atoms vibrated upwards, allowing Jesus to walk on the surface?"

"Everybody knows the Bible is full of miracle stories. The Jews lived in a story-telling culture. Do you really believe the Genesis myth? Do you believe the making of Eve from a rib taken from Adam's side, or the serpent?"

"Suppose Detective Olerhy, you dropped your gun on the floor and it is next to your feet. Let's say in a drunken stupor you shout 'Gun, I command you to rise to my hand,' and lord have mercy, the gun jumps off the ground and lands in your hand! Would that be magic, detective, because it is a violation of a physical law?"

"Like you said, I would have to be in a drunken stupor to believe something like that, and maybe you would have to be too!"

"That is the force that can defy gravity and lift a man up to the ceiling and hang him. What I call black magic!"

"I don't know what to think about Miles's death. I certainly do not believe in the *hocus-pocus* you are talking about. I have never before seen a case in my 20-year career so puzzling. That's why we are ruling it a suicide."

"Detective Olerhy," Mama Laveeza said harshly. "Somethings are best let alone!"

"Like Miles's death?"

"Yes, because there are forces in the universe that you have absolutely no clue about. I have tried to show you, that with subatomic particles, ghosts, spooks, and spiritual entities can all exist on an electromagnetic wavelength that is not perceptible to humans. Dogs, cats, and birds can see these entities, but not humans. It's like cable television. You have to turn on the right wavelength frequency to see the show."

"Okay," Olerhy said, wanting closure. "So you agree his death should be ruled as a suicide?"

"Not if you can explain why leaves turn orange in autumn?"

A shard of moonlight crisscrossed the store window. Her faced looked demonic. Evil. A succubus. Tank started to tap on the window outside, telling him to hurry up.

"Enough talk, follow me detective!"

He entered a twelve-by-twelve room. Hundreds of candles lit the room, and the smell of ganja and incense engulfed the space. He gazed at a blue plastered cracked wall; Greek and Egyptian symbols and hieroglyphics were written on it, like some ancient code. A five-pointed star was drawn on the floor with blue chalk.

It was the same star that was under Miles's hanging body. The smell of jasmine, lilac, and rose from the incense wafted past his nose. Inside the pantagramic circled star were two stools and a small black cauldron filled with bones, vials, feathers, and a man's silver ring that had the letter 'M' engraved on it. He wondered was it Mile's ring? White rose petals lay all about the floor. Mama Laveeza walked to the middle of the circle. She got down on her knees, cuffed her hands as if praying then closed her eyes and started uttering unintelligible invocations. She chanted:

I am Mama Laveeza.

I am a Voodoo priestess.

I am serf and king.

I cure the tears of the heartsick,

when I come near they all sing.

Down to the grave will I take thee.

Out from the noise of strife,

then shalt thou see me death,

then, no longer but life!

"That was by Paul Laurence Dunbar. He was a genius. But now is the time, detective, to show you my magic." She turned around on the floor to face him. Her wolf-gray eyes shone wide and wild. Detective Olerhy unsnapped his holster and slowly gripped his gun. Mama Laveeza folded her legs into a Buddha position and raised her palms toward the ceiling. She lowered both hands into a large vase and picked up a pig fetus and dipped it into a bowl of toad blood, tomb dust, the urine of an unbaptized baby, the nectar from a hemlock plant, and twigs of witch hazel. She dipped the fetus repeatedly into the unholy stew.

"Detective Olerhy, to survive in this insane asylum of steel and concrete we call America, one must seek salvation to justify your existence. My salvation is black magic!"

She picked up the mummified *Bast* sarcophagus and dipped it into the holy stew. Olerhy panicked and pulled out his gun, pointing it at her.

"Stop the carnival bullshit. Enough is enough!"

He watched her as she started to float off the floor. She was levitating. She started chanting with a musical, almost gospel inflection.

"There are mysterious powers that help us fulfill our spiritual purpose in life. You whites have science. Black people have Voodoo and black magic!"

She continued to levitate. He gazed up at her with disbelief. It was the same feeling he had when he saw a magic act, yet he could sense a powerful palpable force in the room that was real. He thought to himself, *the only thing missing is the tortured Rachmaninoff grand piano solo.*

"The earth is a living thing, Mr. Olerhy," she said as her head almost bumped the ceiling. "It is more than oil, diamonds, and gold." A blue mist smoked underneath the door and filled the room. Olerhy walked to the door to open it, but it was locked. The mist slowly formed into the shape of a creature. It was shadowy, with the upper body of a man and the lower body of a goat. The shadowy creature whispered to her, "Damballa is at your command!"

"Show him how Miles died!" Mama Laveeza shouted as she descended from the ceiling. Detective Olerhy strained his eyes as the creature's chest opened up like a window. It showed a Gargoyle-like creature hoisting Miles Malone up to the ceiling pipe, defying gravity, and Mama Laveeza was standing with arms folded hovering about two feet above the white roses. Then suddenly the creature and image vanished.

"My magic killed Miles Malone. He was a killer, he deserved to die!" She hackled as Detective Olerhy turned on the lights and held his gun tightly.

"Good show Miss Betty Laveeza, but I can see the same act in Las Vegas much faster and I still don't…."

She had vanished. He turned the doorknob once more and this time the door opened. He walked out of the room and the entire shop was in pitch black. He pulled out his gun as he banged into tables and chairs blindly. Suddenly, he heard a beastly howl. He started running toward the front door; he could see the moon through the blinds. Then he heard the scratching of claws as they struck the slippery floor. He ran faster; he looked back and saw a huge two-headed she-wolf monster on all fours, knocking over furniture and heading toward him. Its huge wolf head had sapphire eyes. Its large fangs dripped saliva.

"Do you believe now Detective Olerhy!?" Mama Laveeza growled as his hand quickly opened the front door and slammed it behind him, holding the doorknob tightly out of fear.

"Damn man, what the hell hit the door like that? She got a dog. You act like you seen a ghost Olerhy!" Tank smiled.

"You wouldn't believe it if I said I did. Give me a cigarette and let's go get a bottle of Johnny Walker Red."

- ◊ -

FAMOUS BLUES SINGER FOUND

HANGED IN MOTHER'S APARTMENT

By Phillip Carlson

Miles Malone, a 55-year-old famous blues guitarist, was going to be charged on Monday with the killing of Mary Lee Laveeza, whose body was found in a basement furnace last week. Detectives found her room and the basement awash in blood. Forensic evidence and Miles Malone's prints on the murder weapon and his bloody guitar placed him at the scene of the crime.

Detective Milton Olerhy said him and his partner, Detective Joe Morgan, found Miles Malone's body hanging at his mother's Southside apartment building at 8:30 p.m. when they were out to issue his arrest. Authorities are baffled in determining how he could have hanged himself without any visible means of reaching a 10-foot high ceiling heat pipe and tying a rope around his neck, and then putting his head in a noose. His death has been ruled a suicide.

HEX

HANGAR 17

Southampton, Virginia

January 2007

"Hello, this is James Whitley. I'm a writer for the Chicago Defender newspaper. Can I speak to Mr. David Lewis please?"

"Just a minute," a woman with a slight lisp answered.

"Lewis...telephone! It's some newspaperman from Chicago." She spoke to James; "he will be right with you son!"

"Thanks, are you his wife?" I noticed the musical inflection in her voice, a Southern accent.

"Yes, we just celebrated our 60th anniversary. We married in 1947. I just had my 80th birthday and Lewis celebrated his 82nd."

"Congratulations to you both."

"Thank you, God has really blessed us."

The sound of John Coltrane's "*My favorite Things*" echoed in the background. It made me think about how Voyager 1 and 2 were launched 30 years ago, with a time capsule that carried a phonograph record and a 12-inch, gold-plated disk containing songs selected by Dr. Carl Sagan. Songs like "*Johnny B. Goode,*" by Chuck Benny, "*Melancholy Blues,*" by Louis Armstrong, and "*Dark Was The Night,*" by Blind Willie Johnson. It will be 40,000 years before that package makes a close approach to any other planet system.

My thoughts vanished when a ragged voice wheezed into the phone.

"I'm Mr. Lewis. Can I help you son?"

"Mr. Lewis, my name is James Whitley and I'm writing a story about the 1947 UFO crash that occurred in Roswell in New Mexico. You were the only black military person that was a firsthand witness to the case. I would like to talk to you about your view of what you saw. Would it be possible for you to interview with me? I'll be in town until tomorrow evening."

A hopeless silence rose between us. It was so quiet you could've heard a roach crawl across a pillow.

"For the past 60 years -" he coughed, swished his mouth, and the sound of something hitting a nearby can echoed down the earpiece.

"Are you alright, Mr. Lewis?

"Yes, thank ya' son, I've been smoking all my life. Anyway, the USAF, NSA, the FBI and the CIA have killed people for talking about that crash. The U.S. government wants to keep the case classified to keep the public from panicking. So they had to silence us with the threat of death. But there is another price you pay for not telling the truth." There was a pause, and James thought the old man had hung up. "But fuck it, I'm ready to die and I want my story told!" he finished.

"It would be a great honor for you to share your story with me, Sir," I said.

"Make it about 4 p.m., we should be back from church by then. And I won't change my mind."

"See you then Mr. Lewis, and thanks."

I wondered if any story was worth a man's life - even mine. I drove back to my hotel thinking about what Mr. David Lewis said about publishing his information about the Roswell UFO crash, and how it could be life-threatening. I had conducted phone interviews with people who had first- and second-hand knowledge of the *"crash."* They said that everyone that broke the code of silence had died mysterious deaths.

Once I got back to my hotel room, I scanned a report named TOP-SECRET UMBRA, which was approved for release by NSA on 11-03-2005 pursuant to E.O 12958, as amended:

TOP-SECRET UMBRA
UNITED STATED DISTRICT COURT
FOR THE DISTRICT OF COLUMBIA

CITIZENS AGAINST UNIDENTIFIED

FLYING OBJECTS SECRECY

Plaintiff,
V.
NATIONAL SECURITY AGENCY,
Defendant.
Civil Action No. 80-1562

IN CAMERA
AFFIDAVIT OF EUGENE F. YEATES

County of Anne Arundel
ss: State of Maryland
Eugene F. Yeates, being duly sworn, deposes and says:

1. *U) I am the Chief, Office of Policy, of the National Security Agency (NSA)> As Chief, Office of Policy, I'm responsible for processing all initial requests made pursuant to the Freedom of Information Act (FOIA) for NSA records.......*

After I read the so-called TOP-SECRET UMBRA report, I tossed it in the garbage. It was too obfuscated. The letters "U", "C", "S", and "TS" indicated whether the information is unclassified or is classified as confidential, secret or top secret.

I knew from my research that Sergeant Dale Lewis, the only black man at the scene along with his redheaded captain, threatened a mortician at Ballard's funeral home, who also drove one of Roswell's ambulances. After driving an injured soldier to the base, I heard through an interview that Sergeant Lewis instructed a sheriff to tell Dennis to keep quiet or his Army fighter pilot brothers would be benched. I put down my notes, made a Scotch and soda, and wondered what tomorrow's interview with Mr. Lewis would reveal. Most Americans believed the Roswell crash was one of the defining moments in UFO history. Whether Mr. Lewis's secret would put closure on the case was quite another matter.

January 3, 2007

After eating turnip greens, candy yams, meatloaf, cornbread, and ice-cold lemonade, Mr. Lewis stood, anchoring his gaunt body with his cane, and stooped down to kiss his wife on the forehead. I followed him as he hobbled into his living room. His wife winked at me, giving me the nod of approval. She was a petite woman with olive skin, freckles, and coal black hair sprinkled with grey, which she tied into a ponytail. It had the sheer and texture of a Cherokee squaw. Her face was stenciled with lines of age, yet when she smiled, her pearly teeth beamed a youthful inner soul.

Mr. Lewis was dark brown in complexion and he had a large hooknose that was lighter than the rest of his face. It looked like a bird's beak. Patches of grey hair sprouted from his head like wild weeds. His face was cadaverous, shrunken, and etched with wrinkled lines telling a full life. The whites of his eyes had an enameled yellow tint, jaundice-like. There was a musty odor that seemed to float through the house. It was the stench of age and decaying flesh. He sat down on an old, brown leather couch. His snarled hands picked up a pipe off the table. He lit it and gazed at me through cloudy glasses from the bluish haze of tobacco smoke.

Bright orange sunrays burned through the living room windows: the walls lay home to pictures of President Harry Truman, one of a blond, blue-eyed Jesus kneeling and gazing at a cobalt blue sky; pictures of his children, grandchildren, and a picture of him when he was a young sergeant.

Suddenly, a white poodle hopped on the sofa next to him. He rubbed it and whispered *Lee Lee*. The dog lapped his hand, revealing brown, rotten teeth. A sliver of sunlight showed spots of pink underneath its wrinkled coat. For a nanosecond they both looked surreal, like they were stuffed and on display at the "Death around the Corner Museum."

"Tell me about yourself boy. Are you a veteran?"

"I'm a graduate of Morehouse College. My major was in journalism. I'm married and have two young sons. I'm not a veteran, but my father is an ex-Marine. He fought in Vietnam during the Tet' Offensive."

"Look son," the old man croaked as he relit his pipe. "The information you want could be life-threatening. Think about your wife and kids' safety. This house could be bugged. The government has *killed* over this case. It's too late for an old fart like me, but you're young…"

"I understand Mr. Lewis, but sometimes you live for one defining moment in your life. This is mine."

"Alright, I'm going to tell you something that no one will believe. But I want you to promise me that what I tell you will be written just as I tell you, agreed?"

"I agree. Can I turn on the tape recorder now, Mr. Lewis?"

"Let's get started."

I clicked on the recorder and placed it on the short coffee table between us. Mr. Lewis cleared his throat roughly.

"Son, do you believe in God?" He began.

"Yes, I do."

"Well, make sure you include this in the interview. In the New Testament, one verse implies that the existence of life on other planets is true. It says, and I quote, *"Go ye into all the world and preach the Gospel to every creature."* Son, the key word is "world" in original Greek; it means 'Kosmos.'"

"I agree that there is God that governs the universe, not just earth. Do you remember Glynn Dennis? He was a mortician that worked for Ballard Funeral Home in Roswell, New Mexico."

"Yeah, I remember him," Mr. Lewis thought. "He was not only a mortician, but he was an ambulance driver for the base. He was a nosy cocky SOB. That's what got him into trouble. You see, the base mortuary officer had already phoned Ballard's Funeral Home in Roswell asking Dennis about the size, type, and hermet… what's that word?"

"Hermetically?" I offered.

"Yes, that's it - hermetically sealed caskets. Years later, Dennis admitted that he thought they were hiding something. In fact, a nurse he dated helped perform the autopsy. She even winked at him when he glanced in the autopsy room. He saw the same bodies I did. Two were mutilated and one was injured, but alive. I knew Dr. Jesse R. Thompson, Jr. He was assigned to Squadron M, South Bomb Group and was the base pathologist - he died mysteriously, along with the nurse and other doctor before they could be contacted about their autopsies."

"What did the alien look like?" I asked.

"They had huge fuckin' heads, like watermelons. When I was a kid we would call them water heads. They had large Asian-shaped eyes, no eyelids, and their mouths were just a tiny slit. No ears, and their arms were long and ape-like. They had tiny holes for the nose and hands that had four fingers, with no thumbs. There was webbing between the fingers, like those between an octopus's tentacles. They were pinkish-gray in color. The skin was ribbed, scaly, lizard like. They didn't seem to have any genitals. They were small, like midgets, about 4 foot, 3 inches. Dr. Thompson told me they didn't have red blood like ours, but a clear fluid. They had no digestive systems, no asshole; they were seriously weird."

"So Glen Dennis accidentally stumbled upon the autopsy room?"

"Officer Rick Peterson, the Chief Intelligence Officer of the 500th Bomb Group of the Eighth Air Force Army Air Field -- what we call *RAAF*-- spotted him and asked who he was, and what he was doing there. Dennis told him he was from Ballard Funeral Home, then the idiot said 'looks like you had a crash.' That's when Officer Peterson told two burly MPs to get him out of there—fast."

I watched Mr. Lewis shift about in his seat uncomfortably. He coughed again, clearing his throat.

"Where were you at while this was happening, Mr. Lewis?" I asked.

"I was down the hallway, writing instructions about Hangar 17 on my clipboard. I was the in NCOIC in charge at the time. Remember, this was before President Harry Truman desegregated the armed forces in 1948. I was handpicked to become a radio operator when I first enlisted.

"During World War II, our forces were spread thin across the Pacific Rim and the U.S. military needed a way to encrypt our radio codes with a non-military one. I was selected along with Navajo Indians who used their language, which is so complex a single word can convey a whole sentence. The Navajo language could not be understood by German or Japanese operators who happened to intercept them. I was used to add military code words and black American slang like *bebop*, which made it impossible for their Nazi and Japanese engineers to unscramble our signals.

"You see, I was the only cryptographer on base at Roswell after the UFO crash. Captain Petersen wanted me to try to decode the bizarre symbols forming a border around part of the outside of the crashed ship—it reminded me of geometrics or hieroglyphics."

"Did you break the code, Mr. Lewis?" I asked, eagerly. I could sense we were getting somewhere.

"No, the symbols were not of this planet."

"You mean symbols of an alien culture?"

"You sure you are a Morehouse grad? I said *muthafuckin* UFO!"

I laughed. "So what happened next?"

"I sent the symbols to my old team who had helped develop the Colossus electrical digital computer that helped with cracking the German Enigma Signals. The Colossus team included academics, chess players, crossword puzzle solvers, mathematicians, and even brilliant jazz musicians—we still couldn't decipher the symbols."

"What happened next with Dennis?"

"Captain Petersen called him an SOB. Said he wasn't through with him. Two MPs grabbed him and brought him back to us. Captain Petersen shouted at him that there was no crash. That he didn't see anything. He told him that if he valued his life and love ones, he couldn't talk to anyone about what had – or hadn't – seen."

"What did Dennis say?"

"He told the captain to go to hell because he was a civilian. That's when both of us lashed out at him. The captain told us to be quiet or somebody would be picking our bones out of the sand. I told him he'd be helping daisy's grow! You should have seen the look on his face. Dennis turned stone white." He chuckled lightly to himself, reminiscing.

"You mentioned earlier that you were talking to Captain Petersen about Hangar 17. Can you tell me more about that?"

"The captain sent me and two MPs to Magdalena, on the outskirts in San Agustin near Socorro, New Mexico, about 100 miles west of Roswell. There was an abandoned Hangar 17 out there. A guy by the name of Grady Tarnet - I think he was some kind of dirt engineer - told us he saw a crashed saucer with small aliens with midget-like bodies, with big heads, slanted eyes—some lying dead and others standing alive outside the crashed UFO. We were to go out there and secure the site to take the bodies to Hangar 17. Later the bodies would be taken to Wright Patterson, where a secret 'Hangar 18' complex housed alien crafts and remains under a code name called 'PROJECT X.'"

"When you got there, what happened?" Mr. Lewis paused. The air held the silence as I waited in anticipation.

"This is the part of the story no one will believe - that's why you must, I repeat you must, write what I say, understand?"

"Yes, of course I will, but what were the MPs names? The two MPs who were with you?"

"They died mysteriously without telling a soul about what we saw. I prefer not to mention their names."

"What did you see when you got to the crash site?"

"We saw the smashed saucer, but no dead aliens. There was a burning cross right next to the wreck."

"Are you shittin' me?" I asked, incredulously. "A burning cross, like the one Jesus was crucified on?"

"No, more like the Klu Klux Klan used to terrorize black folks."

"Mr. Lewis, we are talking about New Mexico, not Selma, Alabama or Mississippi. New Mexico ain't the *Deep* South!"

Hangar 17

"I told you no one would believe me. But I have proof; I have pictures to prove it. Nobody else has ever seen them in the past 60 years. Not even my wife."

"Can I see them, sir?"

"Yes, I'll show you them, just as soon as I have finished my story. "We followed a trail of tracks that led to Hangar 17. When we got there, we saw four pickup trucks. We pulled out our weapons and crept up to the hangar's windows. We couldn't believe what we saw inside…three aliens were hanging from chains tied to rafters. We also saw a few ranchers, civilians and robed KKK shouting and hooting like they were at a horse or slave auction. They were bidding over the body parts of the aliens. I guess they thought the body parts would make them rich and might serve well as souvenirs for family and friends.

"They saw us, obviously, and tied us with rope and duct tape, leaving us there to die.

"How did you get away?"

"One of the MPs broke loose and freed us. He was an amateur photographer. He sent me copies from the photographic plates before they were confiscated from him. The photos were of the two aliens that were lynched in Hangar 17."

"Did you say *lynched?*"

"Yes, but a picture is better than a thousand words; I'll be right back."

David Lewis stood slowly, using his cane as an anchor. He limped down the hallway and I heard the thump of boxes hitting the floor. I thought about how historic events are often shrouded in secrecy, and how that a black man seeing the lynching of aliens could be one of the major historic events of the last thousand years.

I wondered if the world was ready for my story. Would they believe it? That was why the photos were critical as hard evidence. Lightning started to flash through the window. The rat-a-tat of rain started beating on the windowpanes. Mr. Lewis limped back into the living room, holding a manila envelope and a small black box. He sat down and gestured for me to sit next to him.

"You can shut off your recorder now son," he smiled and handed me the envelope. "That photo and what's in the black box will make you a wealthy man. But before you open it," he paused and patted me on the knee. "Let me tell you something about myself. I was born in Richmond, Virginia, but I grew up here in Southampton County. I remember when I was growing up, how William McKee and I were as tight as sardines - we were the best of friends! We went to the same school, lived in the same black section of Southampton. We even joined the Army together.

"We went to the Southampton's Bicentennial Celebration; I never will forget how dark and ominous the sky became that day. As William and I entered the armory looking for girls, we wandered between stalls and displays of paintings, flowers, fruits and vegetables, stuffed birds, buffalo heads, caged rats, rabbits, puppies, dried squids, and bottled lighting bugs. We laughed at the weird people that were selling their wares at the market. We suddenly stopped and looked at something on a table that looked like human skin. William noticed a dark brown purse in a large glass container, stating that it had been made with the skin of Nat Turner and it was priced at $10,000."

"You mean the Nat Turner who killed all those whites during his slave revolt in about 1831?"

"Yes, that's the Nat. He was hanged in Jerusalem, in Southampton County, which is not far from here. He was hung on November 11, 1831. When I was growing up here, it was a rite of passage to remember that Nat waited for a sign of God before he told his followers to prepare for revolt. It was supposed to happen on the Fourth of July, but he was sick.

"Son, I remember a time right here in Southampton, how after a lynching that black fingers would be preserved and displayed in jars…just like what is in that black box. It's no different than the purse made from Nat Turner's skin. The same hatred was behind those barbaric acts. Now, you can look at the photo and open the box."

I opened the clasped manila envelope and pulled out a glossy 8X10-color photo of the lynching. I was astonished.

It showed the dead aliens, the Klan, and the ranchers that lynched them. It also showed men looking into the camera.

"Open the box now, son," Mr. Lewis said, a toothless grin etched on his face, as if the box contained the secret to salvation and immortality, as if it contained the Holy Grail.

"Go on son, open it."

To me the box was a microcosm of modernity's fetish to have zoos, museums, bazaars, department stores, and shop windows all designed to display commodity - like whatever was inside the box. It was one of those felt boxes that would have slots in them for rings. I opened the box. A mildewed odor seeped from it - it smelled like the animal cages at Lincoln Park Zoo in Chicago that I went to in my youth.

My hand shook the box nervously as I looked at the curled, knotted, snared finger inside. It was like looking at an anatomical specimen at a museum. It was a symbol of the white man's power to collect and examine things; to commodity. The dissection of the alien was like an exhibition; a dissection and display of Cuvier's on comparative anatomy.

The fluid underneath the fold between the fingers had a dim florescent glow. The finger looked like a squid tentacle you could buy at the meat counter. I wondered if Mr. Lewis would let me get a DNA test of the alien's finger. Like Nat Turner's black knuckles, these fingers had been brutally removed from his hands during his lynching and displayed in a butcher shop window in downtown Southampton.

Hangar 17

I snapped the box closed after taking photographs and gave the box back to Mr. Lewis. I shook his hand, and put the tape recorder, manila envelope, and camera inside my attaché case.

I hugged both Mr. Lewis and his wife, and walked into a rain-soaked Virginia night, thinking that the Milky Way galaxy was a distant 100,000 light years across; and there are stars older than our g-type sun, which harbor planets like Earth. It means there has to be advanced civilizations out there. I wondered: *Will anybody believe my story, even without the hard evidence, like that alien finger that Mr. Lewis would not let me get DNA test on?*

As I walked toward my car, two men wearing trench coats and fedoras approached me. The white man pulled out a fob with 'Project X' etched on it. The black man spoke to me.

"Mr. Whitley, I think you have something that belongs to the Federal Government in your case."

"What are you talking about?" I asked angrily.

"Mr. Whitley, you have a healthy, beautiful wife and children. Let's keep it that way. Give me the case, now.

As I gave him the case, he unsnapped it, peered inside and nodded to his fellow agent. I saw a light pop on in Mr. Lewis's house. I could see him peeking out of the curtains. I could see the shiny gleam of the barrel of his shotgun.

"Mr. Whitley, this never happened! You must not ever tell anyone about what you have seen and heard. Mr. Lewis is too old to kill. Don't endanger your family over something no one will ever believe, you understand?"

But what I couldn't understand was concealing the defining moment in my career. Either I would be faced with forever keeping the story of the century a secret, or death. But who would believe me anyway?

Do you?

Acknowledgements

Author David B. Lentz for his introduction to "The Color of my Blood". Lunabea and Linda for their brilliant typing, editing and formatting skills. Stephen at Goodreads for his insights and suggestions. And especially to Rev. Branagain Garlick, for his brilliant critique and suggestions. Also to Funygfx for his brilliant video book trailers. To Mdesignz for his brilliant book cover for USS OBAMA, and last but not least, Fantabanner for his incredible e-book covers.

About the Author

John H. Sibley was born in Chicago and lived in Robbins, Illinois, and Aurora. After graduating from Eisenhower high school (he is a hall-of famer!) he studied at the American Academy of Art in Chicago, and then enlisted in the United States Air force in 1968 during the bloody Tet Offensive during the Vietnam Era and served two years in the Pacific Rim. Upon his honorable discharge, he studied at Kennedy & King College on Chicago's Southside and transferred to SAIC, The School of the Art Institute of Chicago, where he achieved his BFA in 1994.

He was briefly a Chicago schoolteacher, and later was hi red in the private sector as a supervisor for a high-tech accoustic company for 27 years. He has two daughters, a son and two grandchildren.

Now recently retired, Sibley continues to pursue his passion of painting and writing full time.

- ◊ -

To see Sibley's art, please visit http://john-sibley.fineartamerica.com

Mr. Sibley is also represented by the Atkinson-O' Rourke Gallery in Elmhurst, Ill—info@aogallery.com

For further books by Sibley, plus access to YouTube videos, please visit: amazon.com/author/johnsibley

Made in the USA
Lexington, KY
14 April 2017